Bread and Chocolate

Philippa Gregory

HarperCollins*Publishers*

HarperCollins*Publishers*
77–85 Fulham Palace Road,
Hammersmith, London W6 8JB

www.harpercollins.co.uk

This paperback edition 2002

First published in Great Britain by HarperCollins*Publishers* 2000

Some of these stories, in slightly different versions, have appeared
in the following publications:
*Living, Woman's Weekly, You Magazine, Woman & Home,
Candis* and *Good Food Magazine*

ISBN 978-0-00-714589-8

Set in Postscript Linotype Aldus

Mixed Sources
Product group from well-managed
forests and other controlled sources
www.fsc.org Cert no. SW-COC-001806
© 1996 Forest Stewardship Council

FSC is a non-profit international organisation established to promote the
responsible management of the world's forests. Products carrying the FSC
label are independently certified to assure consumers that they come
from forests that are managed to meet the social, economic and
ecological needs of present and future generations.

Find out more about HarperCollins and the environment at
www.harpercollins.co.uk/green

For Anthony

Contents

Bread and Chocolate

The sun streamed through the windows set in the vaulted whitewashed ceiling high above Brother James's head. The golden light illuminated the cloud of flour drifting upwards from his working hands, danced on the dough and was kneaded into the mix along with a whispered prayer and the live pungent yeast. He divided the great body of bread into eight equal pieces and set them to one side, covered in warm tea towels to rise. The scent of yeast and clean cloth filled the high kitchen.

An arched door opened and one of the younger brothers stuck his tonsured head into the room. Brother James looked up, irritated at the interruption.

'Father Pierce says you are to go to him.'

Brother James threw one anxious glance towards his rising bread but obeyed the greater imperative. He rubbed his hands, enjoying the familiar pleasure of dry dough peeling from skin, washed them under the tap, dried them on a towel hung in front of the huge monastery cooker and, still wearing his crisp white apron, strode down the length of the kitchen aisle. At the far end, as distant as possible, the young vegetable cook was slicing an avalanche of courgettes.

'May I see to the bread?'

'No!' Brother James snapped. 'Leave it alone.'

He reproved himself for lack of charity as he shut the door on his brother's crestfallen face. But he cheered up almost immediately. Any man who obeyed the rules of poverty, chastity, and obedience, daily and without fail, might allow himself the occasional human error of grumpiness, especially to some damned carrot peeler.

'It's about your book,' Father Pierce said without preamble.

Brother James stood before the huge carved desk, his head slightly bowed to signify his absolute obedience.

'I have a letter here from the publishers. Turns out it's doing rather well. They want to reprint it.'

A flicker of what might have been pride gleamed for a moment in Brother James's face and was instantly repressed.

'People are keen on cookbooks,' the abbot remarked. 'And they say that your bread recipes and the spiritual element are exactly right for . . .' He consulted the letter '. . . the gourmet new-hippie market.' He looked at Brother James over his severe horn-rimmed glasses. 'Gourmet new-hippie? I thought it was just bread recipes with a few prayers.'

'It is,' Brother James said modestly.

'They want you to do a programme for the television,'

Father Pierce remarked. 'Show people how to cook the bread, I suppose. They want to film our daily life here, and then cut to the studio kitchen where you will be making our bread.'

'Cut?'

'Should I say slice?'

Brother James shook his head. 'They want me on the television?'

Father Pierce consulted the letter again, he was enjoying himself. 'They say that if you are sufficiently televisual they could promise you two programmes, and perhaps a new career as a presenter.' His solemn demeanour cracked and he laughed aloud. 'They seem to have no notion that you *have* a career. They seem to think you are employed as a cook here. They don't understand that your vocation is to God, and that you bake bread as part of your service to the community.'

'And what will you tell them?' Brother James asked.

'You have no preferences?' the abbot questioned acutely.

The younger man bowed his head. 'I obey, Father Pierce,' he said simply.

The abbot thought for a moment. He did not tell the Brother Breadmaker that the fee offered at the foot of the letter would pay for installing central heating in the chapel, a sum for which he had been praying nightly. 'I think you should do it,' he said. 'God speaks in many tongues. Perhaps He is calling you to teach those who ask for a stone and can be given bread.'

❖

'And who will make the bread for the brothers while I am away?' Brother James asked.

'Your assistant? Brother Gervase?'

'I will bake extra and freeze it. He can be trusted to defrost,' Brother James said glacially. 'Nothing more.'

'You should be training him,' the abbot reminded him gently.

'I am trying to.' Brother James bowed and went from the room.

His abbot watched him go. 'And perhaps the outside world may teach you, Brother James.'

The arrival of the film crew at Wentworth Monastery was watched by the noviciates from the high window of their dormitory in a state of explosive excitement. The television set was only unveiled at the monastery on occasions of high national solemnity: a royal wedding, a royal funeral, a general election or the outbreak of war. The rest of the time it was shrouded in a purple pall, like an unwanted chalice, and wheeled into a cupboard in the refectory. But now television itself was coming to Wentworth Monastery, was thrusting itself in with lights and cables and vans and cameras and a small crane and track and a mobile generator.

'When you have finished hanging out of the window like a coach-load of schoolgirls I should be glad to see you in chapel,' the choirmaster observed sourly from the door of the noviciates' dormitory. 'And if I catch one, just one, young man looking towards the camera or behaving in any way as if his mind were not on the words of his service then there will be a choir practice which lasts until the middle of next week. You are to behave as if they are not there. And any man of any sense would be wishing they were not.'

Brother James, torn between vanity and embarrassment, could not behave as if they were not there. They crept behind him with a huge camera in a nightmarish game of grandmother's footsteps. Every time he paused and looked around, the great square dark eye would be peering at him, looking over his shoulder into the mixing bowl, flinching back from the splash of breaking eggs, dollying forward to catch the gleam of water drops on a toast-brown crust, a duster wildly polishing away the glaze of steam from a loaf newly emerged from the oven.

'This is just actuality, lovey,' the director assured him.

Brother James cast one furious look at the young vegetable chef who had never heard one of the brotherhood called 'lovey' before.

'When we get you in studio we'll get in much closer. Some really luscious close-ups. This is just to show you in your natural environment. Tomorrow we'll have you all to ourselves.'

The vegetable chef kept his head down and sliced with devotion.

'D'you have another – er – gown?' the director asked. 'As a bit of a change? One for best?'

Brother James looked down at the brown habit and the

white rope belt, the white apron overall. 'No,' he said shortly.

'We could run you one up. You'd suit blue.'

Brother James hesitated, unsure how to express revulsion. 'No,' he said simply.

The director took him familiarly by the sleeve. 'Don't get me wrong, you look terrific. But we have a natural wood set, very nice, built just for you, very Gothic you know? And I thought you'd look wonderful behind the pine wood table in blue. I *saw* you in blue.'

Brother James unclasped the fingers and stepped away. 'This is the colour of my order,' he said gently. 'It is part of my vow of obedience to wear it. I could not wear anything else.'

'Oh.' The director was taken aback. 'Can't they let you off, just for once?'

'I have made a vow, a solemn vow, of poverty, obedience and celibacy,' Brother James told him firmly. 'There is no "let-off".'

The director looked at him in amazement. 'You've promised to be poor? To be obedient? And don't tell me you never –'

It was too much for the vegetable chef. With a wail he dropped his knife and fled from the kitchen.

They took Brother James to the television studio in a long limousine. He sat awkwardly in the back hugging a big box of bread ingredients and his favourite mixing bowl, spoons, and bread tins. He did not release the box until they showed him to the table in the corner of the studio which they had dressed as a monastery kitchen.

'Is this absolutely right?' asked the assistant director, a waif-like girl swathed completely in black, peering through her glasses. 'Just like the monastery?'

'I don't have a crucifix hanging over the cooker,' Brother James remarked.

'No? OK.' She turned her head. 'Kill the crucifix – I mean – sorry, er, Mr James – take the crucifix down.'

'You call me Brother James,' he said mildly.

She looked pleased. 'I'm Liz. Can I leave the Bible in shot?'

'I don't read the Bible in the kitchen,' he said.

'OK. OK. But we wanted something to show the spiritual element. You say in your book that you bless the bread before you start baking. Would that be with holy water? Or an incense burner – one of those, whatd'youcallit, censers – or something?'

Brother James felt unaccountably weary. 'I just ask for a blessing on the work,' he said. 'This is bread that is going to feed my brothers. It should be made with love and respect.'

That stopped her for a moment. 'That's really neat,' she said. 'Really neat. And I guess you don't need incense to do that?'

'No.'

She glanced at her clipboard. 'You're a segment,' she

told him. 'We'll do you, and the rising dough, and then we'll cut away to Caroline. She's going to do sensual puddings. She's doing Devil's Food Cake – a sort of a joke, you see – holy bread and sinful puddings. Then we'll come back to you for the final kneading and putting the dough in. Then at the end of the programme we'll see you take the bread out of the oven and break it and say grace. You do say grace, don't you?'

He nodded.

'I'll introduce you to Caroline,' she said. She hesitated. 'She can be a little – a little difficult sometimes. But I'm sure you'll get on wonderfully well.'

He put on his apron and tied the straps around his waist. He felt safer with the armour of stiff white linen around him, and the familiar scent of the clean cloth.

A woman was threading through the confusion of the studio, coming towards them. Unlike everyone else she was not wearing blue denim or washed-out black. She was wearing a deep purple suit, dark as a Victoria plum. The skirt dropped, slim as a spatula, to her knees; the matching jacket swung like an archbishop's cape as she strode towards him, her hips swaying, her paces long. Her hair was thick: dark and lustrous as liquorice; her eyes brown as chocolate, her mouth a sulky kissable bud, stained as if she had been eating blackcurrant jam.

She had come to complain to the assistant director about a slight, about an oversight, about something wrong with the layout of her table, of the preparation of the Devil's

Food Cake, but when she raised her long eyelashes and saw Brother James she paused.

'Oh,' she said.

And Brother James, holding tight to his mixing bowl and his wooden spoon, for the first time in his life looked desire in the face and longed to taste.

'Oh,' he replied.

Caroline Davis put out a manicured hand to Brother James. 'How do you do?'

Her voice was warm and smooth, as if she had been drinking the chocolate she so liberally applied to her famous puddings.

'You must think this place is a mad house.'

'It's very different from the monastery,' he said shortly.

'I bet. What sort of bread are you making?'

It was the first time that anyone had asked him about his work. He could not help but warm to her.

'I don't know,' he confessed. 'I brought the ingredients for everything. I bake plain bread and bread rolls every day for the brothers, and I thought it might be simple and honest to start with a white bread. But we have some wonderful celebration breads with fruit and nuts, and I wanted to share them too. We have corn breads, and sourdough breads . . .'

'Show me the recipes,' she commanded. Suddenly she was brisk and helpful and businesslike. He opened his looseleaf folder and watched her read.

'This is a treasury,' she remarked.

❖

'It matters to me,' he volunteered. 'It's a staple food, of course. But it's more than that. Our Lord named himself as bread. He ordered us to pray for our daily bread. I serve my brothers when I bake for them.'

'How did you learn? Where did you get all these recipes?'

'I was taught by a brother baker. And I will teach my apprentice. The skills are handed down, the recipes too.'

'I can't teach. I don't have the patience,' she remarked.

He remembered with a flicker of guilt the disappointed face of Brother Gervase. 'I mean I will teach my apprentice,' he promised himself. 'Some time.'

One recipe she rejected at once, pointing out that it would be hard for him to prepare in the time allowed. Another was rejected on the grounds that it would not film well.

'It's not how it tastes in television cookery,' she said dismissively. 'We can all stand around saying: "Oh, how delicious!" It's how it looks that counts. It's how you look while you cook it that counts.'

He hesitated. 'Where I come from it is never how things look. It is always how they are.'

She gave him a quick sweet smile. 'This is the outside world now, Brother James. This is all surface, a world of meringue, not meat.'

The assistant director hovered and then approached. 'Time to go to makeup,' she said to Brother James.

'Don't be a complete fool,' Caroline Davis said sharply. 'He's as handsome as a Greek god. What d'you want to do? Give him lip gloss?' To James she turned and said reassuringly, 'Be yourself. Nothing else is more important,' and then she was gone.

Brother James watched her stride away to the other side of the studio and snap at the assistant cook who was unpacking ingredients from cling-filmed bowls.

'Was she all right?' the assistant director asked nervously.

'Wonderful,' he said.

He cooked a plain peasant bread as she had recommended and became absorbed, as he always did, in the familiar comfort of kneading the dough, feeling it come alive under his fingers, under the heel of his hand, the transformation of individual ingredients into the wonderful elasticity of dough with its hidden life which would warm and swell under the secret shield of the tea towel.

When the camera crew moved in a rush from his table to Caroline's he went with them and watched her long fingers pointing at the ingredients, deftly spooning the glutinous shining body of chocolate batter, as rounded and gleaming as a slug. And then came the little miracle of television cookery – the arrival of the perfectly cooked dish at the very moment it was needed. She spun on her heel to the eye-level cooker and produced a cake at the very second of perfection. Smoothly she turned it out on to a wire rack, and it slid from the tin keeping its perfect shape: a sponge as light as air, as dark as lust. He could smell the hot cake from where he was standing and he felt the saliva rush into his mouth like a presentiment of sin.

The assistant director had to nudge him to rush back to his own mock-Gothic pine table to bring the loaves out of the oven and to break the bread as part of the closing credits. His bread was golden and wholesome with a toast-brown crust. He broke it before the dark observing eye of the camera and smelt the familiar scent of home.

'Well done,' Caroline Davis said as the film crew were clearing up. There was a tradition that the food cooked for the programme was shared out with a glass of wine. She offered him a slice of her Devil's Food Cake. 'D'you want a taste?' she asked.

He took a paper plate and plastic fork. The icing was as dark and moist and heavenly sweet as the cake itself. The first forkful adhered to the roof of his mouth in a melting mass. He closed his eyes in pleasure. When he opened them he saw that she was watching him with a cool measuring gaze.

'Stay behind,' she said quietly. 'When all this lot have gone. Stay behind and we'll have a glass of wine on our own.'

'They've ordered a car to take me back –'

'It'll wait.'

The crew thinned out, disappeared. Someone said a whispered word to Caroline and she snapped at him and then the two of them were left alone in the darkness of the studio which was as cavernous and quiet as an empty cathedral, with only the two altars of the cooking tables illuminated. Caroline drew closer to him and put her slim hand on the white bib of his apron. 'You are quite, quite fascinating,' she said very quietly.

He knew himself to be in great moral danger. 'Why did you want me to stay?' he asked.

Her gaze did not waver. 'I imagine you know why. I felt – didn't you? – an instant attraction.'

He cleared his throat. 'I am not available for instant attractions,' he said clumsily. 'Nor, er, lasting ones. I have given my life to . . .'

'D'you know,' she interrupted him before he could speak his refusal, 'I think I must taste of chocolate.' She turned her face towards him so close that he could feel her warm breath on his lips. He smelled her: the scent of a woman, a heady mixture of warm makeup, perfume, her liquorice hair, her vanilla skin, and the deep erotic odour of chocolate. He was lost.

'I never saw such a rich sponge that was so light,' he gabbled. 'Will you show me how you did it?'

She was diverted for a moment, then she laughed. 'You must pay me,' she said. 'I don't work without a fee.'

'I don't have any . . . my vows are obedience, poverty and . . . and . . .'

'Pay me with a kiss.'

They brought Brother James back to the monastery by limousine, still holding his large box of ingredients and utensils. His apron, still crisply white, was folded on top of the box. Brother Gervase was waiting at the door to greet him.

'Did you use the frozen bread?' Brother James demanded without a word of greeting. 'Did it defrost all right?'

'Yes, Brother. I did just as you said. We all saw you on the television. It was a wonderful programme, Brother. And the cake! Brother Jerome said you could make it for us for Easter – that chocolate cake that the woman made.'

'I might,' Brother James said grudgingly.

The young man led the way into their shared kitchen. Brother James hesitated on the threshold. At his marble top, where he, and he alone, always made the monastery's bread there was already a fine dusting of flour and the shrouded bowls of rising loaves. He turned on the younger brother with a face like thunder.

'I thought you wouldn't mind if I started some rolls for the brothers' dinner,' the young man stammered. 'I so want to learn, Brother James. I so want you to teach me!'

Brother James placed the box heavily on the wooden worktop and strode to his breadmaking board. He shook out his apron with an outraged flourish and tied it on like a warrior girding himself for battle. Then he hesitated. The dough was well kneaded, the yeast was worked evenly through the cream-coloured mixture. It was rising in pleasing rounded shapes. It would be good bread.

His anger and sense of intrusion died away. The brother was young and had a right to learn his trade. Perhaps he had been too hard on the lad. A little charity should always have a place in a well-run kitchen. And no-one is perfect. He smelled the intoxicating smell of warm yeast, the smell of fertile female life itself filling the kitchen with its warmth. No-one can promise to be perfect, we all need forgiveness for one sin or another.

'Brother James? Shall I fetch you a clean apron?'

Brother James glanced down at the immaculate white of his starched apron and then gasped. In the very centre, dark against the whiteness, was the unmistakable cupid's bow outline of a chocolate kiss.

Brother James paused for a moment, remembering something which had been very sweet and very surprising. Like a rich chocolate cake but as light as air.

'Yes,' he said. 'Fetch me a clean apron and we'll make a start.'

Coo-eee

He saw her the moment the bus drew up at the quayside and the doors opened with a hiss into the bright Aegean sunlight and hot Aegean air. She had a scarlet baseball cap crammed on a head of tight permed curls. It said 'Widget Dodgers' above the wide peak, which shaded her pink sun-burned face; a slogan so obscure that he found it lodged in his brain as he watched her labour up the gangplank and haul on the hand of the crew member who waited to wel-come her on board.

'I'm game for a laff, me,' she remarked to no-one in particular when she was landed on deck, and then she looked at him as if he had caught her eye, as she had caught his.

'You'll be the teacher,' she exclaimed. 'Am I right?'

'Guest lecturer,' he murmured.

'I doubt you'll teach anything to me!' she exclaimed, and turned to her husband who bobbed along in her wake. 'I said, I doubt he'll teach anything to me.'

'Certainly not, if you are not interested,' he said

pleasantly. 'It's not school, it's not compulsory. Some people find that a little information enhances their cruise. They like to know a little about the history and background of the scenery. But some people prefer to drift and wonder. Think of me as a bar snack. Nibble or not, as you wish.'

It was a practised speech, not a spontaneous one, and it had always worked before for first-time educational cruise goers who found the thought of a guest lecturer on board too daunting. She barely drew breath before she exploded in a loud honking laugh.

'Nibble! Aye! I like a good nibble!'

To his horror she bared her red lips and showed her pink gums and snapped her white strong teeth at him as if she would gobble him up, then and there, on A deck.

'George'll tell you I like a good nibble when I'm in the mood,' she proclaimed.

The steward diverted her by coming up then with the clipboard to tell them their cabin number. The lecturer was sorry to hear that they were two doors down from his own cabin but he was relieved as they moved away, following the steward. Still he heard her saying: 'Don't I, George? Like a good nibble?', and George's quieter assent, 'Yes Bunny. Yes, dear.'

It was as if each had sighted their own shadow, their own negative, that day at the gangplank: the elegant refined lecturer and the bawdy noisy woman. She was fascinated by him, and he felt both fascinated and repelled by her. She could not leave him alone, she attended his every lecture: Minoan Relics, Etruscan Civilisation, Hellenic Culture. Whatever the title, she was there in the back row: mildly subversive, slightly disorderly. Never exactly heckling – which he would have managed well; he had taught undergraduates all his professional life – but always running a commentary which was so irrelevant or steeped in such ignorance that it defied him to educate her to a better understanding.

She had picked up from somewhere the notion that Oedipus Rex had an unnatural fixation on his mother, and somehow muddled it into the belief that he was, therefore, homosexual. When the lecture concerned the Greek tragedies and referred to Oedipus and the tragic forging of his destiny from the prophecy that he would kill his father and marry his mother, she grew rowdy in the back row. 'I reckon they're a nation of Oedipusses,' she declared of the Greeks. 'Oedipussies, we oughter call them. Nancies, the lot of them. Look at how they carried on in the old days and they're no better now.'

He could feel his temper rising but he kept his voice icy. 'Excuse me, I think you have misunderstood.'

She shook her enormously enlarged head, ignoring him completely. It was a morning lecture and she had come to it wearing her hair rollers with a scarf tied over the top. It was an outfit so bizarre, so ghastly for a prestigious cruise ship that no-one had the courage to challenge her.

'You know what you ought to do?' she counter-attacked.

'You ought to have a bit of a laff. You're too serious. That's why we're all falling asleep. You ought to have a bit of a laff. We're on holiday, us. Not in school. Why, when we went to Egypt last year to see the pyramids and all we had a teacher on board like you but he had a bit of a laff. You learn more that way too. He had funny names for everybody. I can remember them now. So you see it works. He called one of the queens "Hot Chicken Soup", I remember that. And the mummy with all the gold – Tutankhamen, that's him. He called him "Toot-toot". And when he mentioned him we all had to shout out "Toot-toot!" You ought to do that. We'd all remember much more and we'd have a bit of a laff.'

He found he was looking around the lecture room in something like desperation, waiting for someone else to tell her that this was a Hellenic cruise with a guest lecturer, not some kind of music hall turn. In his confusion he saw only stern faces and could not judge whether they disapproved of her or of him. She beamed at him in the silence. 'But go on,' she said. 'It's very interesting. All about this Oedipus Rex. Oedipus Sex, you oughter call him!' She laughed loudly. 'Oedipus Sex!'

He stepped down from the lectern. 'Excuse me,' he said faintly. 'I feel unwell.' He went swiftly from the lecture room, across the bright sunlit deck and down the shady corridor to his cabin. He shut the door behind him and lay on his bunk, his hand over his eyes. For no reason at all that he could think of, he felt seasick for the first time in his life.

After that she was everywhere, as if scenting victory over him. When he talked quietly after dinner to a pleasant table of people about the writing of Homer, with a tiny black Greek coffee before him and a glass of Metaxa at his elbow, she appeared from nowhere bearing a huge frothing glass adorned with little paper umbrellas and streamers.

'Try this,' she ordered, plonking it down before him. 'I got the barman to make it up for you special. I call it the Sexy Rexy. He says you'll have ten per cent of every one he sells. I cut you in on the deal. Don't thank me! Just tell me if you like it?'

He would have demurred but she could overcome any protestation. She could overcome any refusal. He began to fear that nothing could stop her. He drank the drink she ordered for him, she brought him another. He surrendered the after-dinner conversation he was enjoying, she dominated the table.

'Now we're having fun,' she declared and arranged the party into a circle so that they could play charades. He slipped away before he had to hear more than: 'Now then! Sounds like snog', and leaned over the stern rail and watched the small sliver of moon on the edge of the sky and the white wake vanishing into the blackness of the wine-dark sea.

He went to his cabin early, he did not dare to accept an invitation to join a table and talk with them for fear that she would see him and come waddling in, shouting encouragement, and telling people about her trip to Egypt when the lecturer had been such a laff. He took a large glass of brandy with him and sat on his narrow bed and drank it, looking mournfully out of the dark porthole where the islands he loved so much, slept in the darkness of night and forgotten history.

He was starting to get undressed when he heard her unmistakable shriek of laughter at the head of the corridor, and he sank back on his bunk, gritting his teeth at the very presence of her on the far side of his door, weaving her way, probably drunk, to her own cabin just two doors down.

'Bet you I dare!' she cried to her companions.

Shrill giggles alerted him that she was not with the helpless George who normally escorted her everywhere, but with her new friends, two women travelling alone, who had mistaken loudness for confidence, and were eager to hear of her adventures in Egypt and her equally profound knowledge of Indian art.

'Bet you think I don't dare!' she cried again to shrill squeals of delighted alarm, only this time even louder, right outside his cabin.

Ignoring the disturbance, he pulled down his trousers and started to step into his cotton pyjamas. His horror when he saw the door knob turn was total. The door opened and she entered in one smooth movement and slammed it shut behind her with a noise as loud as one of Zeus's thunderbolts. She was inside his cabin and he was a man surprised, with one leg in a pyjama trouser and one leg still out, his nakedness open to her frank scrutiny.

'They dared me!' she said, out of breath. 'So I did.'

She seemed to think that was explanation enough. 'But now I'm here...' She swayed towards him, staggering slightly from the rocking of the ship, her clumsiness exaggerated by the three Sexy Rexys she had drunk. 'Now I'm here – how about a bit of a giggle? Or a bit of a nibble, as you offered? You naughty man! You naughty naughty man!'

She came towards him, as unstoppable as an oil tanker. He shrank back, the narrow cabin bed offering no refuge. Still she came on. He thought wildly of the several hours that it took for a ship to stop at sea, as she surged forwards and fastened her bright wide mouth on his and thrust a cold hand down into the tangle of his clenched pyjamas.

She pulled him out like a bookmark. 'Whassamatter?' she asked. 'You want a little warming up?'

She kissed him again, more insistently, her gin-sweet tongue pressing against his closed lips. 'Come on,' she urged him. 'Let's have a little fun. Let's have a laff.' She reared back and gazed at him unblinkingly. 'If you're worried about George, he's out for the count. Nobody knows I'm here.' She had quite forgotten her bosom pals of the corridor; but he could imagine them, only too vividly, listening to all of this at the door of his cabin, daring each other to bend and peep through the keyhole.

He tried to rise to his feet but his pyjama trousers, one leg on, one leg off, entangled him and he fell back on his single bunk. 'I must ask you to leave,' he said and knew himself to be pompous and powerless.

'Oh, give us a kiss.' Once again she insistently fumbled down the front of his trousers. 'Come on. Warm you up! Cheer you up. Show a girl a good time! Come on!'

He found the strength in his irritation to push her away, and at last got his second foot down the second trouser leg. He pulled the trousers up, tied the cord, and confronted her with more authority. 'You must go,' he said. 'You should never have come in. I did not invite you. Your presence here is a mistake.'

'Whassamatter? You some kind of pansy?' she asked, lurching back from him and bumping against the door. He could not now throw the door open, she was clinging to the door knob for support. 'You some kind of faggot? You some kind of queer? You some kind of Oedipussy? Is that why you're so keen on him?'

'Get out,' he said coldly. 'Get out and I don't want to see you again.'

Roughly he pushed her aside so that he could pull open the door. As soon as it opened her two companions tumbled in as if they were enacting some ghastly farce. He stood, glacial and irritated, as they picked themselves up and got themselves out of his cabin. Only when they were all gone, like reprimanded fourth formers, did he sink to his little bunk bed and put his head in his hands and shake from the horror of it, and from the shame of her questing hand, and from the cruelty of her accusations.

They were at Paxi the next day, an unspoiled Greek island, some few miles from the mainland. There could be nothing here to attract her: a tiny harbour, a boat trip to the Blue Caves, a few quayside bars. Nothing more. He could assume she would stay with the cruise ship, drinking cocktails and looking at the enchanting view of pale rocks and rustling olive groves and complaining of boredom.

'Paxi is principally interesting for the legend that this is where the River Styx flows,' he said as dryly as he could. She was in the back row with George in attendance. She was silent for once. He imagined that a blinding hangover from three Sexy Rexys was suppressing her usual morning vitality.

'The River Styx flows from this mortal world into the underworld, as you know. The only way to the underworld is to be ferried across it by the boatman Charon. It is, as you can imagine, a one-way journey.' He waited for the usual gentle murmur of laughter.

None came. He had lost his audience for this cruise. They were so accustomed to her interpolations of crude jokes that they had lost the taste for mild academic wit. And he had lost his sense of timing. He was no longer confident before them. He was continually waiting for some noisy demand from her table for a joke or for something to cheer them all up. He could hardly hold the floor when he was certain that in a moment, she would be bellowing: 'After all, what I say is: you're a long time dead!'

'Our ship is too big to enter the narrow harbour of Paxi,' he said when he had left a moment for them to laugh, and they had not laughed. 'So we will take one of the ship's launches to pay a brief trip. We will go down the winding and narrow channel to the harbour, and then we will take a short trip to the Blue Caves, returning in time for lunch on board. You may bring cameras and video apparatus, of course. And if I may ask, when we enter the narrow gorge, let us do it in silence. It does have a certain air of mystery, there is a rather special sense of place. Let us be as quiet as we can to enjoy that.'

He had his eye on her. She looked pale under the yellow colour of the fake tan which she applied religiously every morning. 'For those of you who find the morning sun a little bright there is no need to come,' he continued. 'There are better and more interesting sights to be seen later on this trip. This is really nothing more than a little diversion, of interest only to those of you who know the legend of the River Styx and are curious to look at the jaws of death itself – from the comfort of an Aegean Experience launch rather than Charon's boat!'

Again there was no laugh, but she lifted her heavy head and looked at him, across the room. 'It's always dead things with you, isn't it?' she demanded, and he felt the attention of the room shift to her. 'Old things, and dead things. What I say is: it's all a long time ago!'

He forced himself to smile at her. 'It's been my interest, no, my passion, for all my life,' he said. 'And I know of nothing more rewarding than the study of the classics.'

'Oh yeah,' she said as if that confirmed her worst opinion. She winked at her friends. 'I bet you don't.'

'We can go at once,' he said, speaking to his class over the murmur of their comments on this exchange. 'Anyone interested in seeing Paxi and the legendary mouth of River Styx on Deck B at once please.'

He had been certain that she would not come, but she was there in a bright pink top which showed the swell of her midriff and seam-stretchingly-tight white Capri pants. She wore her heated rollers in her hair as was her habit before noon, but today she had tied a bright pink turban on top by way of camouflage. He watched the sailor help her into the neat little launch and saw the way she held the man's gaze and flashed a smile at him as if the man were serving her from desire and not because he was paid to do it.

He said nothing to her, nothing to any of them, as he dropped into the boat himself. He felt as if he was far away from his class, far away from the subject that he loved. He felt as if he would never speak inspiringly of it again.

But he had a job to do. Not a very academically respectable job, not a very well-paying job, but a job which allowed him to come to Greece twice a year, which was more than enough for him who so deeply loved the islands. And sometimes he was able to explain what the place meant to him, how the light that they saw even now on the pale limestone of Paxi was the same that Homer had seen and loved too.

'This is a very special place,' he said softly into the microphone as the launch moved away from the side of the gently rocking ship. 'Greek legend has it that when a man is dead his soul comes down this narrow gorge and is met here, perhaps exactly here, by a dark boat, guided by the boatman Charon. This is the River Styx and no man ever comes back from his silent journey over these dark waters.'

The cliffs were very narrow on either side of the blue lapping water, the olive trees bowed over their reflection at the water's edge, the cypress trees stood like dark exclamation marks on the horizon. There was no sound but the faint puttering of the outboard motor of the launch, and he let the silence linger, wondering if he could hear at the back of it the beat of Charon's oars.

'*COO-EEE!*' He was so startled that he dropped the microphone and it made a loud popping noise as it hit the teak deck. But the noise she made was even louder. '*COO-EEE!*'

She turned around to him, quite unaware of the sudden thudding of his heart. 'No echo,' she complained. 'No echo. I thought you said this place had a famous echo?'

'I said nothing about an echo,' he said in sudden passion. 'I said a lot, a great deal, about this being the very mouth of death itself. And you come here and bellow Coo-eee!'

She gleamed at him and he saw how his anger thrilled

her. It was his defeat in the game she had been playing with him. She had caught him on the raw and thus she had won.

'Ooo!' she said. 'Oooo! Pardon me for breathing!' She turned to her husband. 'He snapped me head off, didn't he?' she asked. George nodded, looking reproachfully at him. 'All I said was Coo-eee. Testing for the echo. And he snapped my head off.'

'I'll have a word,' George said lugubriously. 'With the purser or the captain. Crew can't talk to passengers like that.'

The lecturer turned away, his face burning, he bent to pick up his microphone and looked towards the back of the boat where the wake twisted in the narrow blue channel like a silver corkscrew. Hopeless to try and invoke the dark magic of Charon for these people. Hopeless to try to give them a sense of the fear and the longing for the River Styx. Pointless to talk to them about the belief that once you crossed the river you remembered nothing – for what did she remember anyway?

'I am sorry the microphone is out of order,' he said shortly, and retreated behind the steering wheel where she mouthed: 'Cheer up, it might never happen!' at him.

That night at dinner, as bad luck would have it, she was seated at his table. Officers and lecturers were rotated around the dining room so that guests had a chance to enjoy their company on every night of their voyage. He found he could hardly speak to her with anything resembling civility. He had already had a brief interview with the purser who told him that a complaint had been made by a guest about his inadequacy as a teacher, and worse – his personal rudeness. Pointless to defend himself by saying that the woman was a barbarian; she was a guest on the cruise, her whims must be accommodated. He spent the evening trying to humour her and found himself treated to a lecture on Indian erotic art.

'Mucky buggers,' she said with delight. 'You should see the things we saw on the temple carvings, and smiling all the time like butter wouldn't melt. We were very surprised, George and I, not thinking of Indians like that. As you don't. But I said to George, it just goes to show that it's the quiet ones that are the worst. But I shan't look Mr Patel at the bottom of our road in the face again, I can tell you. Not now I know what I know.'

'Indeed,' he said. 'More wine?'

He had a fancy that the only way to stop this unending flow of the trivial and the obscene was to pour things down her throat. Already she had eaten a huge five-course dinner with coffee and brandy and now he was encouraging her to drink more. If George would only take her to their cabin! But George was muttering about a nice game of cards and she was declaring that she thought she'd have a bit of a dance, and he could see that she would ask him to dance with her and he would have to accept.

'I think I'll call it a Ladies Excuse Me,' she announced

and rose to her feet. 'Because I'm no lady, and I hope you'll excuse me.'

He could feel himself rising, driven by the rigour of good manners, against his will, against his instinct. He could feel his miserable face setting in a rictus of a polite smile. He knew in the very depths of his aching bones that the moment they arrived on the dance floor two equally awful things could happen: either, the band would play a slow dance and he would receive the full weight of her into his arms, and she would thrust her thigh between his legs and press against him, and tickle the back of his neck with her long fingernails, and lean back and smile at him knowingly, supremely confident that he was aroused by this assault instead of miserably longing for the privacy of his bed. Or – and perhaps worse – the band would burst into the Birdie Dance and he would have to flap his arms like wings and wiggle his bottom like a hen while she, the author of his discomforts, would scream with laughter and shout her mantra: 'I love a laff, me.'

But just as he opened his reluctant arms to receive her she checked. Her bronze-stained face went suddenly white, as if with a shock. She recoiled and her hands went to her throat as if she were choking. She let out one honking cry and she fell backwards, tipping up the table and pulling down the tablecloth in a shower of drinks and glasses.

'Fetch the doctor!' he shouted, and knelt to loosen her clothing. It could not be done. Her gown was so low-cut as to be non-existent to the middle of her cleavage. But still she plucked at her throat and cawed like a fallen crow.

The doctor was at her side, taking her pulse, listening for a breath. He started emergency respiration and the band, not knowing what they should do, started a foxtrot, thought better of it and staggered to a stop. The first-aid team came running in with a stretcher, and the doctor and George got either end of her and lifted her like a slumped gaudy sack.

The lecturer followed, like a ghost drawn behind her, longing to know what the end might be. He waited outside the medical centre, smoking a cigarette cadged from a passing crewman, and heard them trying over and over again to start that fatty heart beating in that lazy body. In the end the door opened and the doctor emerged, yellow light spilling out behind him.

'We lost her, I'm afraid,' he said. 'She's sailing down the river.'

And the lecturer, who had never had an unkind thought nor said an unkind word in his life before, threw his head back to the slip of the white moon and called to her soul as she crossed the River Styx:

'COO-EEE.'

The Favour

'Lady Ygraine?'

She stopped at the whisper from the doorway. 'Who's there?' she asked sharply.

A man stepped out of the shadow. Brown hair, brown eyes, a warm appealing smile. 'Me,' he said.

'David,' she said coolly. 'What is it you want? I am on my way to the hall.'

He nodded. Everyone in the castle was invited to feast with the lord and his lady on this night before the tournament. The fighting men would drink deeply, laughing heartily at jokes that were old, at jests which were not funny, hiding from each other the deep coldness of fear that gripped their bellies.

'I wanted a word with you,' he said. 'Several words.'

He put his hand out to draw her towards the doorway where they would be out of sight of the big double doors leading into the hall. She stiffened and drew back.

'David St Pierre, I am not lingering with you on stairways or in darkened doorways,' she said. 'I have to go to dinner. My lady mother will be looking for me and if I am late I will be whipped. You do me no favour by keeping me here.'

He dropped his hand at once and stepped to the side, out of her way.

'I would not have you hurt, sweetheart,' he said quickly.

She gasped at the endearment. 'I'm not your sweetheart,' she whispered fiercely. 'Never will be. David, you know this full well. Why d'you keep tormenting me and teasing yourself with this? You're the poorest knight in the country. Your horse is a laughing stock. Your castle is some tumbled-down ruin God knows where. My lady mother and my father look a good deal higher for me than some poor knight on the Border marches. And you know it.'

He nodded. 'I know it,' he said. 'But I feel . . .'

'Feel!' she said abruptly. 'What have you or I to do with feelings! When I am wed and have three heirs in the cradle I will have time for feelings. But for now I must know obedience to my mother's will and nothing else.'

'You're very young,' he said softly. His voice held a world of tenderness. 'Very young and very lovely. I don't want to see you married to some great lord who will use you, and beat you, and breed sons on you.'

Ygraine tossed her head and the veil from her tall head-dress brushed across his face like the shadow of a kiss. 'What would you have me do?' she asked him. 'What would you have me do? I didn't choose this life, I didn't make it so that men are lords and women their servants.'

'I would have you listen to your heart,' he said. The lilt in his voice was like that of a travelling storyteller. 'I would have you listen to your heart and see if it doesn't bid you to love me, and come to me. And see then whether I would be your master – or whether we would live as two birds in an apple tree.'

She laughed aloud like a child, throwing her head back in genuine amusement. He grinned back at her, watching the light play on her bare throat and pale skin.

'Hedge sparrows in a gorse bush more like,' she said. Her smile to him was suddenly warm. 'I'd die of cold in your hovel and then you'd see sense and wed a girl who could bring you a dowry big enough to rebuild your tower.'

He shook his head, suddenly serious. 'Not me,' he said. 'I shall love only this one time. I shall love only you, in all my life. I love you; and if I can't have you then no other woman will do for me. No other bride, no other love. No-one, from this day onward.'

She was silenced by that pledge, by the seriousness of his tone. 'David?' she said, uncertainly.

'D'you know what I would like?' he asked.

She stepped a little closer to hear his low voice.

'D'you know what I would like above anything else?'

She shook her head, her eyes on his mouth. Their faces were very close.

'I should like to wear your glove on my lance tomorrow at the jousting so that they know, so that they all know, that whatever the hopes of your mother, whatever the usual way of doing things, that you are promised to me and I to you. They can rage then, or they can yield. I should like to carry your favour.' He paused and gave her a little smile. 'It is a fair exchange, Ygraine. You carry my heart.'

'I don't carry it where everyone can see it!' she retorted. 'I would be shamed before the whole castle, David. You're a dreamer. You've been too long in the wilds of the north. You've forgotten what real life is like.'

He nodded. 'But what if we made a new real life? What if we decided on different rules, on marriage for love, on children raised in our home, not sent away for training as you were, as I was?'

She shook her head slowly. 'There's no other life for me,' she said sadly. 'You can have your dreams, my David. But I have to marry as my mother bids me. I never asked for your heart. I never smiled on you more than courtesy commanded.'

He put his hand forward and took her chin. He turned her face up so that she met his eyes. Her eyes were a deep blue, almost violet.

'Liar,' he said tenderly.

The deep crimson blush came up from her neck up to her forehead and died away again, leaving her pale. He saw that her mouth was trembling as if she were about to cry, and he remembered that she was still very young, and that when she had first smiled on him he had been a friend, her only friend in the huge formal castle. And she had been a little girl.

'We were both just children then,' he said quickly. 'You did nothing wrong.'

'I was so lonely,' she said. Her voice was very quiet, he could scarcely hear her.

'I know,' he said. 'You were such a little girl to be sent away to learn your manners. I never knew how they could bear to part with you.'

She flashed a look up at him, he saw her dark eyelashes were wet. 'And you were the scruffiest squire any lord was ever cursed with,' Ygraine said mischievously. 'All legs and darned hose!'

He nodded. 'You were the only one in the castle more scared than me,' he said. 'I used to shrink like a mouse when my lord looked at me.'

'And now?' she asked. 'Now you want to defy him, and defy his lordship my father, and all of them? You want me to love you in defiance of all of them? You've found a lot of courage from somewhere, little squire David.'

He grinned. 'I want us two mice to run away from this great trap. I want to steal you away to my tumble-down castle and show you the great northern skies which stretch forever. I want to take you to the seas where the waves come rolling in higher than a knight on horseback. I want to take you up to the tops of the hills where only the purple heather grows and only the golden eagles are higher. And I want to love you, Ygraine. I want to love you as if there were no such thing as marriage contracts and dowries and laws between a man and a maid. I want to fold you into my heart.'

He broke off. She had been listening to him with her eyes on the stone floor beneath his boots. The silk trailing from her hat trembled slightly. She shook her head.

'No?' he asked.

'No,' she said very softly.

'May I wear your glove inside my breastplate tomorrow?' he asked. 'No-one will know, Ygraine. And I am . . .' He hesitated, then he told her the truth. 'I am afraid.'

She moved towards him at that, a sudden quick movement as if she would have reached for him, and held him, and loved him at last. But there was a rattle from the doorway of the great hall behind them, and she checked herself like a young horse wrenched to one side by a hard rein.

'No,' she said again. 'Let me pass, David.' She stepped past him and went towards the noise and the smoke and the brightness of the great hall where men feasted and drank because tomorrow was the tournament and some of them would be in danger, and many of them would be hurt.

David was unlucky in his draw, he was matched against Sir Mortimor, a great weighty man who had once killed an opponent. David bowed to the lord and then rode past the box where the ladies were sitting. With his helmet under his arm and his brown hair all rumpled he looked very much like the young page who had befriended Ygraine when she had first come to the castle. He was wearing a white surcoat over his armour, Ygraine saw the tiny darn that she had sewn for him at the bottom. Their eyes met and he smiled at her as if he had not a care in the world. She smiled back, a smile of common politeness, from one acquaintance to another. That brief look had told her at once that he was afraid.

If she had heard of a knight who was afraid before jousting she would have called him a coward and despised him. It was not part of the knightly code to know fear. If she had heard of a woman who lingered in a darkened hallway and listened to a young man tell her he loved her she would have called her shameless, and wondered how she dared. Ygraine shook her head. Nothing was as simple as she had been taught.

The sun was very bright on the jousting ground, it flashed on the polished swords of the knights and glared into Ygraine's narrowed eyes. The ladies' box was shielded by a red and white striped awning, underneath it was as hot as a tent. Ygraine's gown was tight, her high conical headdress made her neck stiff. She watched David's horse trot away to the far end of the list. It looked a very long way to ride in the hot sunlight, in full armour. His page gave him his lance and David hefted it easily, testing the balance. There was no glove tied to the head of his lance. There was no glove hidden, tucked inside his breastplate over his heart. In the ladies' box, sitting still, as she had been trained, with her stiff swanlike neck and her aching blank face, Ygraine gave a tiny shrug. She was not allowed to do anything that would damage her chances of marriage. David should have known better than to ask.

Sir Mortimor had a great bay warhorse, which had seen half a dozen battles and a thousand jousting tournaments. His armour was well polished and dented in half a dozen places. He was an old man, more than forty, but hale and red-cheeked as a winter apple. When his squires heaved him up on his horse he guffawed like a master out for a day's wolf-hunting. His surcoat was white with the bright red cross of an old crusader. David, at the other end of the field, put on his helmet. He did not look again towards Ygraine.

'I don't like young St Pierre's chances against Sir Mortimor,' Lady Delby said languidly. The awning over their heads flapped as a sudden cool breeze blew in. It chilled Ygraine.

'Sir Mortimor won't hurt him,' Liza Fielden said comfortably. 'Why, St Pierre is little more than a boy. Knighted only two years, isn't he? Sir Mortimor will just knock him off his horse for the sport.'

'It's a bad matching,' Lady Sara said. 'I don't like to see a young man knocked out. He's a pleasant youth, St Pierre. I've begged my lord to take him into our company often enough.'

'He's an independent young puppy,' Lady Delby said abruptly. 'Disobeying his father's dying wish and refusing to marry, hiding himself in some cold ruin in the Marches for half the year.' She paused and slid a spiteful sideways glance at Ygraine. 'A handsome youth, don't you think, Ygraine?'

Ygraine flushed scarlet but she kept her voice steady. 'I like him well,' she said. 'When I was sent to this castle I was only seven years old, and friendless. He found me when I was lost one day in the woods on the west side. He put me up on his horse and led it home. I was glad of his kindness that day, and others.'

Lady Delby raised her pale eyebrows. 'I'm surprised her ladyship allowed a maid in waiting so much licence,' she said coolly. 'Walking in the woods!'

Ygraine dropped her gaze and said nothing more. The trumpet sounded and his lordship stood in his box. His hand raised the white handkerchief. Ygraine leaned forward to see better. At one end of the list Sir Mortimor held in his heavy warhorse on a tight rein. David St Pierre, in the distance, looked small.

The handkerchief dropped.

Everything happened with extreme slowness, as if the horses were galloping towards each other in a dream, as if the great lances were coming down in a formal elegant dance. The crowds, even the nobility in the boxes, rose slowly to their feet. The big warhorse and the dainty mare thundered towards each other but Ygraine could not hear the sound of the hoofbeats. Sir Mortimor's lance came up, aimed directly at David St Pierre, the seasoned old knight guessing that David would swerve to one side. But David rode straight at him, with a high fine courage, which had the poor people cheering. David's lance smacked into the knight's chest, shivered on impact, snapped. Sir Mortimor's lance belted the younger man in the belly like a fist. Slowly, slowly, fatally, David was lifted, on the point of the lance, out of his saddle.

Ygraine saw him rise, saw the mare check in confusion at the loss of her rider, then heard the jolting clatter and crash of David's cheap thin armour as he thudded to the earth at the feet of the big bay horse.

'Sweet lady, is he dead?' Lady Fielden exclaimed.

Lady Delby crossed herself, her lips moving silently.

'Dead?' Ygraine asked. It was as if she had heard the word for the first time, as if she were turning the meaning of it over in her mind. 'Dead?'

Lady Fielden shot a quick look back at Ygraine, and her sharp eyes narrowed when she saw the girl's face. 'Not a word more,' she said in a sharp undertone. 'Ygraine, the sun is troubling me, give me your arm back to the castle. I am going to my room to rest. This is poor sport here.'

Ygraine turned a tranced white face towards her. 'Dead?' she asked.

'Come,' Lady Fielden said abruptly. 'Take my arm, Ygraine.'

Ygraine rose to her feet but turned away from the older woman, as if she would go out to the jousting ground itself. 'I must go to him,' she said. 'He wanted to wear my glove on his lance and I said "no". He wanted to hide it inside his armour and I said "no" to that too. Anything he wanted, any little thing, I denied him them all.'

'Quite right,' said Liza Fielden sharply. 'Now come away!'

Ygraine took two stumbling steps, then she looked back. David's squire had his master's helmet off. David's curly brown head lay on the grass. He was quite still.

'Is he dead?' Ygraine asked incredulously.

Liza Fielden gripped Ygraine's arm and drew her out of the ladies' box, through the crowd which parted to let them through, up the stone steps of the terraced garden and in through the wide open doors of the castle to the darkness and coldness inside.

As soon as the shade fell on Ygraine's blank face she whirled around and said 'David!' in a cry like a falcon makes when it has lost sight of the falconer and is lost in a strange country.

'Hush!' Lady Fielden hissed at her. 'You will be ruined, Ygraine. Hush and come away to my rooms.'

She half-dragged the girl through the great hall, empty now except for two large dogs nosing among the rushes on the floor, and up the turret staircase. Only when she had pushed Ygraine roughly into the room and bolted the door behind them did the woman loosen her grip on the girl's arm.

Ygraine touched her arm as if she had been hurt. She looked with wide lost eyes at Liza Fielden. 'Why did you take me away from him?' she asked. 'He's dead now, isn't he? My reputation is safe enough with a corpse, isn't it? I could tell him now that I love him, can't I? Now that he can't hear me? I'm allowed to kiss his face now he can't feel it? Aren't I? Now that he will never hold me, and never kiss me. I can love him *now*, can't I?'

Liza Fielden slowly shook her head. She crossed to the window seat and sat down by the slit window. Looking down she could see them carrying David St Pierre's body, awkward and limp on a long shield. They were taking him to the chapel. Some friend would sit in vigil with the body all night long, and tomorrow they would bury him. Ygraine had no time for vigil. She must bury her loss this day, and smile and laugh and show herself ready for her mother's order to marry a stranger.

'No, you cannot love him now,' Liza Fielden said with a sigh. 'Not even now, Ygraine. You did well to hide your love all these years while you have been growing up. But you're a woman now, and a woman may love no-one but her lord. Not even a boy who died before he could hold her. Your love is dead, Ygraine, forget it; forget him.'

She had thought the girl would flare up. She was almost disappointed when Ygraine looked at her blankly, and then the anger went out of her dark blue eyes and was replaced by the look that cattle wear, when they are walking slowly to the butcher's yard. Ygraine's passion had been under the yoke of obedience for so long that she could forget if she were ordered to forget. And the dangerous love which Liza Fielden had watched grow, and which she had envied, was over. Ygraine was as cold as David St Pierre when they laid him on the marble stone in the chapel and put a candle at his head and another at his feet.

When Liza Fielden's women came in a flurry of excitement to sit with her, she nodded to Ygraine and told them to brew her a tisane of poppy-seed, and let her lie and sleep for she had been wearied by the sun in the brightness of the morning. One girl hid her mouth with her hand and whispered a word to another. Liza Fielden raked her with a look and the girl was silent. Ygraine slept as if she never wanted to wake.

They laughed a little less at dinner that night. It was still noisy – men shouting for meat or more ale, hammering at the table with the bone handles of their meat daggers, tripping the hurrying pages, throwing scraps to the dogs. But David St Pierre's place was empty, and they left a seat and a plate for him, out of respect. His best friend, another young impoverished knight from the desolate northern moorlands, was absent too – sitting away the long cold hours at David's side.

The ladies' table was quieter, the women chatted in an undertone, trying to speak of something other than jousting, or David, or Ygraine. For Ygraine was missing. Her mother was tight-lipped and bright-eyed. Liza Fielden sat beside her and spun some tale about Ygraine and the sun shining too bright. But the women were as avid as adders for a drink in hot weather. The women knew. They knew

Ygraine had loved him, but they had thought she had curbed herself on a tight rein, kept silent, lowered her eyes, bated her breath. Now she was missing from dinner and her lady mother was black as thunder beside the empty place.

Ygraine would be whipped, Ygraine would be ruined unless she came to dinner at once, and talked and smiled at once. Half of them thought she would never manage it – playacting fit for a mummer's show. All of them knew she *had* to do it. Their eyes were as bright as cats' hunting at night. Their gentle voices were rippling with an unstated excitement. They looked as if they had taken the fever, they were hot for her disgrace. And among them, with a look that would freeze water, sat Ygraine's mother. A woman with a hard hand, and other daughters to dispose of too.

There was a rustle at the tapestry which hung across the little door to the hall and the women glanced over. In their sudden silence the noise made by the shouting men was abrupt and loud; and then they were quiet too. No-one could believe what they were seeing.

It was the Lady Ygraine, her head held high like a bride, as pale as a ghost; but smiling a little private smile, as if she were walking to meet her lover. Her hair was gathered under her tall hat, the silk veil streamed out behind her. Her gown was pale green, a colour like birch leaves in springtime. And over her gown she wore David St Pierre's surcoat; with the mud on the back where he had fallen, and the bloodstain very crimson on the front. She walked quietly to the ladies' table and took her place, her eyes cast down as a modest maiden should sit.

'Ygraine!' her mother hissed urgently. 'What the devil are you doing, girl!'

And the Lady Ygraine, grown at last from the little girl whom David St Pierre had loved, met her mother's appalled face with a smile as clear as birdsong on a summer morning. 'I am wearing my lord's favour as he would wish,' she said. 'For he carried me in his heart, even on the very day of his death.'

Theories About Men

❖

When Stephanie was only thirty years old, and married only five years, she evolved her own theories about men. She believed that men are unfaithful to their wives not from passion, but from an innate vagueness that they can no more help than the month of November can help being wintry. Husbands simply forget that they are married and monogamous. She had a theory that wives always lose on divorce: a smaller house, less than half the income, and a scarcity of attractive men. She had a theory that marriages are never ended by the single fact of infidelity, but by the long corrosive negotiations after the discovery. And she had a theory that if a clever woman discovered her husband had strayed, she might be able to get him back by confidently acting as if the whole affair had never taken place. Her theory was that men are creatures of habit, and that the habit of coming home to the same comfortable house every night is stronger than the appeal of running around. Especially after the novelty has worn off.

When she was forty-one, and sixteen years married, she

had the doubtful pleasure of putting her theories to the test.

Her husband Jeff was an estate agent, a partner in his father's profitable company. On their marriage his father had given them the deposit money for a large house set in a spacious garden in Kent. It was the house that Stephanie had wanted all her life: a Victorian residence with a wide double door and a generous sweep of stairs. Stephanie, who had been brought up in the poorer parts of Rye, had looked at houses like that and always longed for their style, and their implied stability. It was her desire to be in houses like that, if only as a visitor, that had drawn her into the estate agency business, first as a secretary, and then as a junior agent. It was her desire to own a house like that which had prompted her to fall in love with Jeff.

They married, and were given their house, and Stephanie left her job. It was thought undignified to have the daughter-in-law of the director trekking around from one little house to another, and haggling for her share of the commission. Instead, Stephanie took a cordon bleu cook's course, read with careful attention books on interior design and home-making, and devoted herself to the comfort and convenience of her husband. She cooked breakfast and dinner for him every day of his life, she maintained the house, she drove for him, she acted as his secretary, she kept the books of the company and typed confidential documents. She gardened, she remembered his parents' birthdays and anniversaries, she returned rented videos on time, she paid the bills before they were red, she never overdrew on her housekeeping account. In short she was a highly skilled professional wife and she regarded her unceasing work as a fair return for the house she had always wanted.

When she fell out of love with Jeff, which happened quite soon, she was careful to conceal the change in her feelings; since she never fell out of love with the house.

In summer she always served dinner for the two of them in the conservatory. One evening in July it was warm enough to open the doors to the warm, sweet-smelling twilight. She had chilled two bottles of rather good white wine and Jeff was drinking heavily. As Stephanie rose to clear the pudding dishes he suddenly said: 'Leave that. I have to talk to you about something.'

At the sound of his troubled voice her first thought was of bankruptcy. These were difficult times for all business, two friends had husbands out of work and – much worse – had been forced to sell their lovely houses, and put the large solid furniture into store. She worked on the company account books every week and they all seemed well; but Stephanie's first fear would always be the loss of her home.

'I don't know how to tell you,' he said. 'I don't know where to begin. You must have noticed that I'm different!' He looked at her hopefully and she thought at once that he was ill and that she had failed him by not noticing symptoms. Her father-in-law would blame her, and she would feel that the investment made in her – the garden, the precious house – had been fraudulently obtained.

Guiltily she sank back into her seat and shook her head.

'How can I tell you?' He drew a breath. 'I've been seeing someone,' he said. 'Oh God. Seeing someone. It's been a year now. I've hated lying. I love her. I have to live with her.'

He broke off, looking at Stephanie for some kind of response. She could feel her face freezing into stillness.

'We've tried,' Jeff said.

Stephanie mutely registered that this 'we' was a new one. It no longer meant her and Jeff. It now meant Jeff and this woman.

'What's her name?' she asked.

He looked at her suspiciously, as if she were taking evidence against him. 'Elizabeth,' he said. 'We tried not to see each other. We tried to stop. It's hopeless. I cannot live without her.'

Stephanie saw the gleam of pride on his face before he dropped his head into his hands.

'You are in love,' she observed.

His head was up in a moment. 'I knew you would understand,' he said. 'It's never been like this for me before. I can't help myself. I have to be with her. I've been in hell these last three months. You must have seen it.'

Stephanie thought of the last three months. June had been wonderful for roses in the garden, every Saturday they had given little summer dinner parties with iced fruit puddings, and there had been fresh roses in every room in the house. May had been disappointingly wet. Her father-

[52]

in-law had wanted some confidential reports typed, and she had spent days with the rain streaming down the windows, in the cold spare bedroom, tactfully amending his sadly inaccurate spelling. She had lifted all the tulip bulbs in April and it had taken nearly a week to dig and store them all. Of Jeff's anguish she had no recollection at all.

'I don't remember,' she said honestly.

Jeff looked a little aggrieved. 'I've been dreading telling you. But I'll take care of you, of course. I'll get you a nice place in town, a smaller house would be less work and you could get a job again. Maybe a flat, and then you'd not have to bother with a garden at all. How many bulbs did you plant last autumn? It was practically a full-time job. Elizabeth says –' He broke off, remembering just in time that Elizabeth's detailed analyses of his wife had better not be repeated.

Stephanie blinked. She very badly wanted to take the pudding dishes to the dishwasher before the cream dried on them.

'But I like living here,' she said. Even to her own ears she sounded defeated. 'I like living here with you,' she added hoping for a more personal note.

He shook his head with a new certainty – these were Elizabeth's certainties. 'I'm not the man for you. I know it now. You need someone who's more like you: a home-lover. Not a wheeler-dealer, running around every day like me. You're wasted on me, I can see that now.'

Stephanie absorbed another of Elizabeth's considered

opinions in silence. Until now she had thought her husband was a rather dull copy of his father. It had been Jeffrey Davidson Senior who had built the company, who had put it at the top in the small market town, who told his son what to do. But apparently – in Elizabeth's version – Jeff was some kind of financial wizard, and she was a slow housewife, holding him back.

'I see.' She was remembering, and it was scant comfort, that she had always believed that male fidelity was an act of convenience, not of conviction. Now it seemed that it was more convenient for Jeff to leave his wife than stay with her.

'What shall we do?' she asked. She could hear panic rising in her voice. 'What does your father say?'

'He likes Elizabeth. He thinks she's a real go-getter.'

Stephanie nodded at this description – an unfortunate one since Elizabeth had gone and got Stephanie's husband. But if Jeff's father was giving the affair his blessing then Stephanie was in real danger.

'What work does she do?'

'She's a personnel consultant. She came to do the sackings at the office last year.'

'And what do you plan?'

'I've had a word with our lawyer and he'll represent you in an amicable settlement. I'll give you a new house outright, and an allowance, a generous allowance. You won't lose out.'

Stephanie looked out across her garden. In the darkening

trees the blackbirds were calling, settling for the night. A single thrush, high in the copper beech tree was singing, a long warbling call, its breast gilded by the last rays of the sun. Later there would be little bats swooping low through the soft dusk, and owls calling. She could smell the roses she had planted sixteen years ago, their scent lying heavily on the still evening air. 'And you will live here with Elizabeth?'

'She's seen the house. She likes it very much. She says she can really make something out of it.'

'Will you excuse me for a moment?' Stephanie asked. She cleared the pudding plates into the dishwasher, switched it on, and then went up the stairs to their bedroom. She sat before the kidney-shaped dressing table and adjusted the wings of the mirror so that she could see her profile on each side, a dozen versions of her shrinking into infinity.

She could imagine the house that Jeff and his father would think suitable for an estranged wife. It would be a small terraced house in a quiet street near the town centre so that she did not need a car. It might be a two-bedroomed flat in an anonymous block near, but not on, the seafront. It would not be a turn of the century family home in mature wooded gardens.

'No,' she said softly. She took up her hairbrush and gently brushed her bobbed hair. 'Not in a million years,' she said firmly.

She rose from the table and glanced around the room.

◆

In the evening sunlight the room glowed in rose and gold. The wallpaper matched the curtains, which echoed the colours of the carpet. The whole room, indeed the whole house, had that attractive English country look which appears so delightfully easy and yet is so hard to achieve, and time-consuming to maintain.

Stephanie went downstairs again. Jeff had poured himself a large brandy as if in celebration, and was still seated at the table.

'You must do whatever you wish,' she said.

'I thought I'd stay with Elizabeth until you move out.'

She nodded. 'You'll want me to pack for you, then.'

'I'll pack,' Jeff said awkwardly. It would be the first time in sixteen years that he had packed his own bag.

Stephanie nodded and let him go upstairs into their bedroom. She heard him opening and closing cupboard doors, looking for the suitcases. She wiped down the kitchen worktops and then laid the table for breakfast, with a white tablecloth and white napkins. She laid two places, she thought it looked more poignant. Then she went up the stairs and found Jeff thrusting ironed shirts into his suitcase.

'I'll do that,' she offered.

Automatically, he stepped back, but then he hesitated. 'You shouldn't,' he said, embarrassed.

'Why ever not? You'll only get them crumpled, and Elizabeth will have to iron them again.'

He forgot his tragic face and laughed. 'I don't think she'll do that!'

'How inconvenient for you. You'll have to use the laundry service and I hear they're dreadfully careless.'

He flung himself on to the little stool before her dressing table, and glanced at his handsome face in the mirror. 'I can't bear this,' he said dramatically.

'Poor Jeff,' she said sympathetically, folding his shirts carefully and neatly. 'I do hope you're doing the right thing.'

There was a brief silence.

'I thought you would be distraught,' he said.

Only Stephanie could have heard the faint note of disappointment in his voice.

'Of course I am,' she said. 'But it doesn't seem real. What shall we do about dinner with the Mitchells on Friday night?'

He hesitated, and then found the right tone. 'I have lost it all,' he said. 'All! I know it. Our marriage, our friends, everything!'

She nodded. 'If that's what you want, darling.' She was distracted by the sock drawer. 'D'you want enough socks for a week, or do you want to take them all?'

'Just enough ... all of them ...' His outflung gesture implied his despair. 'I can't *think* about socks at a time like this!'

'No,' she said. 'Everything does seem terribly wrong, doesn't it? It doesn't feel like a good idea at all.'

'Oh, but it is,' Jeff said hastily. 'I love her, I can't help myself. I've never ...'

'And all your winter suits?' she interrupted. 'They've all been dry cleaned, of course.'

'You'll miss the house,' he said, trying to invoke her distress.

'Oh, of course. But it's *such* hard work. The garden alone is two days every week. Does Elizabeth garden?'

'No,' he said moodily.

'You'll have to get a gardener then,' she said. 'I'll find a good one and leave Elizabeth a note. They're dreadfully expensive. It'll be about £80 a week. And a housekeeper on top of that.'

'A housekeeper? What will we want a housekeeper for?'

She turned her guileless face to him. 'Elizabeth isn't going to want to do dusting and cleaning at the end of a day's work, is she? All that exhausting sacking of people that she must do? And shopping and cooking dinner, and your breakfast, surely?'

'Well, no . . . but . . .'

'I'll leave you the number of an agency. They're about ten pounds an hour, you'll need someone to come in for at least three hours a day . . .' She started folding his jackets and laying them carefully on top of the suitcase. 'Say six days a week . . . gracious! That's £180 a week. And the gardener as well. That's £260 a week, um, more than £1000 a month. Darling, this is going to be *fearfully* expensive. Are you sure you can afford it?'

Jeff looked anxious. He hated spending money.

'But Elizabeth will help, I'm sure.' She took a gamble. 'Is she *very* well paid?'

'Not yet,' he admitted reluctantly. 'She's a freelance.'

Stephanie looked despondent. 'She won't do the secretarial work and the book-keeping then?'

He shook his head.

'Can she type at least?' Stephanie inquired brightly.

Again he shook his head. 'Another £100,' Stephanie said sadly. She thought for a moment. 'That's £360 a week, that's £18,000 a year that it's going to cost you when you don't have me to work for free. And then you'll have to buy a house for me, plus an allowance.' She looked concerned. 'Surely the business can't stand these extra costs?' She closed the suitcase and clicked the locks shut. 'I think that's all. Do you want me to cancel the Mitchells? What shall I tell them?'

He was reeling at her arithmetic. He had not thought her work was so valuable. 'I'll come,' he said. 'Let's not rush into anything. Don't tell anyone yet.'

She did not show any relief. 'Whatever you like,' she said. 'I'll see you at seven o'clock on Friday. Remind Elizabeth to top up the windscreen washer on your car.'

He looked uneasy. 'I'll do it,' he said. 'It'll be good for me to do my own chores!'

She looked at him blankly. 'Why should you? When you work so hard all day you need a comfortable supportive home. I'm sure Elizabeth feels that. After all she loves you, doesn't she?'

'Oh yes!' he said quickly. 'But she's not the domestic type . . . she's . . . she's a *modern* girl. Liberated.'

Stephanie looked shocked. 'Oh! You poor darling!'

She had to keep her nerve. She stood at the handsome front door and waved until the car was out of sight as she had always done. Her theory was that he would be bored of domestic chaos and hard work within the month.

On Friday Jeff came home to take her to the Mitchells' dinner party. He looked tired, as a man will look who is deeply sexually gratified for the first time in his life. But he also looked shabby.

'Your shoes!' Stephanie exclaimed as he stepped into the hall.

If he had said then, 'Oh, who cares about shoes?', Stephanie would have known that she had lost him forever. But a quick look of irritation crossed his face. 'She said she'd done them,' he said. 'She said she'd do them, if I changed the sheets.'

'Slip them off,' Stephanie said in a tone like honey. 'She's not even touched them. There's a pitcher of chilled martini waiting for you in the sitting room. I'll have to clean these before you can go anywhere.'

He looked at her black cocktail dress. 'You can't polish shoes in that,' he said.

She shrugged her shoulders. 'Black doesn't show the dirt, darling,' she said easily. 'You have a nice drink and relax.'

She saw his face as he turned towards the sitting room,

the log fire, and the pitcher of iced martini with conden-
sation clouding the wet sides of the jug, and the crystal
goblets filled with ice and carefully serrated slices of lime.
There were home-made cheese straws on a plate on the
coffee table and a bowl of home-roasted almonds. He had
the sneaky gleeful look of a man escaping from one house,
to another where he secretly prefers to be.

It was the first time Stephanie had seen that expression
on her husband's face. She thought Elizabeth would have
known it once, but Elizabeth would see it no more.

And she knew that her theories about men had been
right.

Lady Emily's Swim

❖

Lady Emily swam the length of the pool with a slow weary breast stroke. Her face, tipped back to protect her makeup, floated like a dusty Venetian mask above the oily waters. Other bathers in their self-appointed routines paced her, overtook her, lapped her. Lady Emily's steady froggy movements never faltered, she never swerved. When two foolish young men splashed exuberantly near her she shot them a blue look from under her heavy eyelids that was as powerful as a searchlight over a rolling swell. They apologised wetly and porpoised off to the shallow end to try to outswim each other underwater. Lady Emily never broke her stroke, swam on.

Every morning she came to the little health club attached to the hotel. Every morning she swam her twenty lengths with the regularity of a turning waterwheel. Every morning she would mount the steps from the pool, pick up her towel, delicately pat her damp powdered face (leaving brown smears on the club's towel) and saunter to the ladies' changing room.

She never stopped to talk. 'They call it a club, but it isn't really. They just let in anyone. You never know who you might find there.' She never used the other facilities – the sauna: 'so hot!', the steam room: 'stifling!', or the jacuzzi: 'a quite disgusting invention!'

Once a week, on Wednesday, she took the train to London, first class, non-smoker, window seat, facing engine, to have her hair washed and set by Simon at Mayfair who was the only person who had the least idea how to do it. On Thursday it was the Women's Institute market where Lady Emily would buy home-made scones and jars of other women's marmalade and feed her vanity like a hungry butterfly on the flit from cake stall to jam stall: 'Oh Lady Emily! Good morning!' 'Six cheese scones, Lady Emily? Of course!'

Tuesdays, Lady Emily spent at home. In the old days, before the war, when Lady Emily had been nothing more than a Hon. Miss Emily, and the youngest and the plainest of four, being At Home had meant something. Maids in their best caps with streamers served sandwiches and china tea on the lawn under the cedar tree, in the summer which went on and on. Now when Lady Emily was At Home she sat alone and listened to the radio. No-one came to see her. She might as well not have been At Home at all.

Friday was Lady Emily's day for shopping and she had lunch at the Copper Kettle tea rooms where Tracey kept her the window table for twelve o'clock. Tracey was a funny girl, quite hopeless of course, with no more idea of waiting at table than flying to the moon; but she made much of Lady Emily, and, on showing her to her table would say loudly: 'This way, your ladyship.' And if there were tourists in the tea room she would say with special emphasis: 'Here you are, YOUR LADYSHIP. YOUR LADYSHIP's usual table', and Lady Emily would take her seat and glance complacently around to see people staring with that ingratiating half-smile that the English use to show respect for their betters.

Saturday was gardening and perhaps church flower rota day. Sunday was church at eleven and lunch at one, and the *Sunday Telegraph*. 'Don't put the magazine in Lady Emily's,' the newsagent cautioned the boy with dreadful emphasis. 'She doesn't like it.'

Mondays were the worst.

There wasn't really anything for Mondays. Sometimes she would write letters, but she was not a woman to whom words came easily, and she had no friends who wanted to know how she was. Sometimes she would change her library books on Monday. She always borrowed travel books or detective stories for those were the books chosen by her late husband, Sir William, dead so long ago that all that remained of him on this earth was the order for the *Sunday Telegraph* and his widow's limited reading.

Lady Emily did not like reading. She could never remember the clues in order to identify the murderer in the mysteries, and she disliked travel books. One place is, after all, much the same as another, and the authors were so full of

[65]

themselves as if they were brave or clever to go – as if they hadn't chosen to go of their own free will in the first place!

But there is a limit to how long you can spend in a library and not look as if you are one of those pathetic old people with nothing to do, and no friends.

Sometimes on Mondays she telephoned Margaret, her daughter who lived in New York. Faintly in the background behind Margaret's very English, slightly alarmed voice, she could hear the hum of foreign air conditioning – or was it the constant roar of traffic in the heart of that great city? Margaret would always ask, 'Is everything all right?', believing that a telephone call from her mother must herald disaster. And Lady Emily would say irritably: 'Yes, yes. Quite all right. But how are *you*?'

She always placed the kitchen timer by the telephone and she would scrupulously set the time to two minutes and forty-five seconds so that she never exceeded a three-minute call. Margaret, miles away, years away, forgetful and bored of her mother, would hear the insistent tick, tick, ticking, behind Lady Emily's account of the vicar, and slugs in the nasturtiums. Margaret would set her teeth on an impatient outburst and wonder, with dull frustration, why the old woman rang at all. And why always Mondays?

Lady Emily watched the pointer of the timer move upwards to the '0' which signified the end of the call and felt her words syncopated by its clicks. She never spoke to Margaret of the empty house and the week of days, and then the weeks, and then the months which stretched interminably ahead. She had no language for the deep pain- ful rhythms of someone speaking the truth. She had only little words to keep pace with the tick, tick, ticking, until the 'ping' when she said – as she always said – hurriedly: 'There are the pips! I have to go!' And hung up – as she always hung up – without saying goodbye.

Margaret had joined a health club in New York. When she heard, among her mother's other mild complaints, that the George Hotel in town had opened a swimming pool of all things, in what used to be the car park, she sent a cheque for Lady Emily's birthday and a card which said: 'Your first year's sub. for the new health club. Enjoy. Enjoy.'

Lady Emily was not at all sure what Margaret meant by 'Enjoy. Enjoy' but she recognised the unmistakable ring of class argot. The tone which said: 'This is slang, but it is slang as it is spoken by the top people.' Emboldened by the sanction of her daughter, and the code of elite speech, Lady Emily arrived at the hotel's newly completed swimming pool and found that she could join without personal applica- tion to the club committee (which she had rather hoped would be required) and without citing Debrett's.

Instead a languid youth in milk-white shorts took her cheque and pushed a towel across the counter to her. 'Open from haight hay hem to haight pee em,' he said. 'Copy of the rules.'

It was not a proper club. Not a proper club at all. It admitted absolutely anybody who arrived at the door with the fee, and all the hotel guests could come pouring into the pool whenever they chose to use it. And many of them had children who squalled miserably in the shallow end.

Still, Lady Emily learned the name of Phil, the languid youth. She taught him to call her 'yer ladyship' rather than 'missis' and started a new routine, grafted readily enough on to the old, of twenty lengths on Monday, after which she went home and wrote letters, twenty lengths on Tuesday, after which she went to the WI market, twenty lengths on Wednesday, after which she took the train to London and Simon said: 'But dahling! your *hair*', twenty lengths on Thursday before she was At Home, twenty lengths before her big shop on Friday, twenty lengths on Saturday before getting down to the garden. Sunday the pool was closed; and anyway it would hardly have been The Thing to swim on a Sunday.

She never swam any stroke but breast stroke. She never tackled her lengths in any style other than her languid progression down the pool and turn, down the pool and turn. She never dipped her face near the green water. Her scalloped chin was held defiantly above the viscous waves, her powdered face as blank as a Noh mask, fringed with the waving fronds of plastic petals which covered her bathing hat. Lady Emily kept her mouth tight shut against the odd lapping wave, closed hermetically in a bow of cerise. Through her pinched nostrils she breathed, in and out, in and out, with the rhythm of her stroke. She never varied, she never hurried. She scissored her way up and down the pool, her white legs bowing wide like nutcrackers and closing again.

She paused once or twice and held on to the side of the pool and looked down at her legs. The underwater lights shone on her old body illuminating the dull black of her swimming costume and the luminous paleness of her legs and arms. Inflated with water her skin looked like that of a young girl. Lady Emily turned back into the water with her smooth rhythmic stroke.

She thought first of all that she was swimming down a deep limpid river, fringed on either side by huge nut-bearing fruit-bearing trees. She could hear the plop of the ripe fruits as they tumbled into the water, and the 'clop' noise of a fish rising to snap at the rosehip-red fruit as it bobbed on the tide. She swam along narrow deep channels, the current beneath bearing her strongly up.

She swam between fronds of ferns, recklessly, fearing nothing. Onward and onward she swam, her heavy-lidded eyes taking in the vivid colours around her: the bright flicker of a stream of butterflies across a flower, the jewelled greenness of a tree frog, as still as if frozen by an enchant-ment on an emerald leaf. She swam past the smiling sleepy jaws of alligators, who turned their crusty heads to watch her go by, and widened their ochre eyes to frighten her. Her breath came a little faster then, but still, steadily through her nose she breathed, steadily she swam, through the deep channels of a mighty tropical river across inland lagoons, along hidden, secretive waterways. Still she swam upstream, carried by the current, the tepid water lapping under her stretched chin.

Above her head, high above her, was the thick canopy of the tropical forest, the sunlight filtering through the dense green leaves. Birds screamed as they flew overhead and Lady Emily could see the brilliant underside of turquoise wings, the scarlet feathers of their bellies, as they scattered in a flock from one roost to another. In one tree, as she swam with her strong measured stroke under the sweeping branches, there was a white-furred dark-faced monkey, dangling from one long arm. Its bright black eyes saw Lady Emily as she floated by; it bounced on the branch and falling leaves spiralled down into the water around her. Lady Emily swam on.

She swam until the water was not salt, but sweet: river water flowing from an inland lake, brackish and warm. She swam up the furtive channels of the mighty flooded river and watched the water change from deep brown to amber to golden; and become warmer. Only after swimming for what seemed like hours and hours, a lifetime, did Lady Emily's waterlogged feet scrabble gently in soft sand, as she stood upright, and waded to the shore.

She was on a little beach, a half-crescent of white sand bordered with the thick tangle of undergrowth. As she paused, uncertain, a tiny snake, brilliantly striped, slithered away from her shadow into the tangle of knotted branches, creepers and roots. Lady Emily crossed her arms over her naked breasts and felt the equatorial sun burn the salty skin of her back.

There was a man in the shadow of the trees, watching her. Lady Emily stepped forward, out of the water, her bare feet moving without fear across the hot sand, stepping without hesitation into the undergrowth to stand before him. Then she lowered her arms and let him see her nakedness.

Wordlessly he stepped towards her and rested his light brown hands on her bare shoulders. At his touch Lady Emily closed her eyes. She felt the softness of his lips on her neck, his caress brush down over her breast, the faint flickering promise of his tongue at her navel, then he bore her down to the ground and his fingers and then his tongue penetrated deep inside her. Lady Emily groaned and twisted her hands in his dark curly hair, pulling him closer and closer. She slid her hands over his shoulders and down his naked back, pulling him up so that she could kiss his wet mouth which tasted of brine and river water. She pulled at his loincloth and it tumbled away. She gave a little moan of desire and opened herself to him, flowing into the rhythm and sounds of lust, moving with him, just as she had swum towards him: with easy purposeful, powerful motions until her muscles clenched and held, and pleasure flooded through her like flood water down a dry river bank.

'Twenty,' Lady Emily said with quiet satisfaction. She heaved herself out of the pool and sat for a moment on the side, feeling the water drain from her thick costume, enjoying the tremor of tiredness in her old body, and the glazed luxurious half-drunk rapture in her mind. She smiled and whispered, like an incantation: 'Enjoy. Enjoy.'

The If Game

◆

'If you were my mistress I'd drive you home and cook your breakfast,' James said. His roguish smile warned her not to take him too seriously. 'We'd go back to your flat, and I'd cook your breakfast for you.'

Before them were two plates of eggs and bacon: the best the canteen could provide. They had both finished their morning shifts – he had been under the hot lights of the television studio, while she worked in the newsroom of the radio station on the floor above. They often met for breakfast, the studios were darkened and quiet in the early winter mornings. A couple of times that winter it had snowed and they had watched the white flakes against the dark sky. Then he had started playing the If game.

'Oh, if I were your mistress I should live in a hotel,' Sarah replied. 'You would come back to my suite and we would have champagne and croissants.'

'I would bring you champagne and croissants to your flat,' he said, making the game more immediate. 'Serve them to you in your bath. D'you have a bath when you get home? I long for one but the twins are nearly always in the bathroom and by the time they're out, I'm caught up with something else.'

'I have a bath and then I have a sleep,' she said. 'There are some benefits to being a single woman.'

'There are no benefits at all to being a married man. I work all the hours God sends, and then I can't get into my own bathroom. The only benefit would be a delicious secret affair with a wonderful mistress.' He looked at her and smiled his wicked smile. 'You.'

'Oh, I think I would like that,' she said. She pushed her plate away and lit a cigarette. She looked at him from under her eyelashes. 'You could pamper me.'

He felt suddenly excited and confident. 'If you were my mistress I should pamper you enormously,' he said. 'Enormously.'

She gave a quick schoolgirl giggle at the double entendre, and he felt more and more certain that soon, she would say 'yes'.

'Well!' he said lightly. He felt the quick rush of adrenaline, like a gambler when he impulsively stakes a fortune on a single number. He was addicted to the thrill of seduction. 'What about tomorrow?'

When she looked up at him he could almost hear the click of the croupier's wheel. 'Champagne,' she stipulated. '*And* croissants.'

'Lanson black label,' he promised.

*　　*　　*

'If you were my wife I should spend all day in bed with you,' he said. 'These early morning shifts are killers.'

They were in Sarah's bed as usual. From the window of her little flat she could see the fat buds of a horse chestnut tree, splitting under the pressure of the bursting leaves. She stroked a finger down the recessed line of his spine.

'If I were your wife I should collect you from the studio and take you home to bed,' she promised.

'Not with a pair of twins in the house,' James said. He got out of bed and stretched. 'If I get this London job, you could move to London too.' He slipped on his shirt and pulled on his trousers. 'I'd only go home at the weekends.'

'If I were your wife I'd keep you where I could see you,' she remarked. She sat up in bed and clasped her knees. Her arms and shoulders were lightly tanned. She had gone to North Africa at the end of February with a girlfriend. She had lain in the sun all day and dreamed of him. She had refused to dance, to drink, or go sailing, with other men because they were not him. She was, instinctively, a faithful woman.

'If you were my wife I'd stay home,' he said with a smile, pulling on his socks. He stepped into his shoes. He kept his aftershave, hairbrush, and deodorant on her dressing table. In her bathroom was his toothbrush, his towelling robe, his favourite soap.

'You're going to the reception tonight, aren't you?' he asked. He slipped his jacket on and smoothed his tie, looking at himself in her mirror once more. His good looks were his career qualifications, he checked them as a clever man might do IQ tests.

'I've been invited,' she said. 'But isn't Miriam coming?'

He shook his head. 'Babysitter crisis,' he said. 'Shall we meet there and go on for dinner? She won't expect me home till late.'

'Lovely,' she said. At once her plans for the day and evening were drastically reshaped. She would wear a different dress, she would skip lunch. She would get her hair done. She would change the sheets on the bed in case he chose to come back after dinner. She was careful to keep the excitement from her voice that the If game had become a game of planning a future together. 'If we were both in London we could get a flat.'

He smiled for her but it was the mirror which caught the glow. 'I don't see why not,' he said. 'We'd have to be discreet, but it could probably be managed. Miriam would never leave Bristol. She's a home-town girl. If I'm going to London it'll have to be alone – or with you.'

Sarah slid from the bed and stood behind him, her arms embracing him, her warm thin body against him. 'With me,' she said fervently. 'With me.'

They rented a small flat in a modern block. He told Miriam he had a place, little more than a bedsit, nothing special. He moved in the day after one of the twins fell off his tricycle. Miriam spent all day and most of the night at the hospital while the doctors X-rayed and then set the boy's broken arm and wrist. James had been forced to pack for himself, and to leave an empty house. 'If I were your wife you'd come first,' Sarah said.

James was soothed by the flat. Sarah had worked hard all weekend. It was furnished in a light airy style, the walls were pale distemper. There was an expensive hi-fi in one corner and a small television. The floors were shiny boards with occasional bright rugs. Sarah had spent the best part of her first month's wages on it. 'If you were my wife we would be lovers first and parents after.' He took her in his arms. 'I think we should christen the bedroom,' he said. 'Don't you?'

That summer was the best time for them. They met as clandestine lovers on Monday night, and they parted with regret on Friday morning. They played house together – cooking exotic and experimental foods, picnicking in the sitting room, breakfasting in bed. James found his new job hard; he made no friends. He was glad to come home to Sarah, who loyally watched his film reports and praised them. She was promoted in the radio newsroom and would often phone him during the day with a tip-off of a story about to break. James thus gained a reputation for being a competent news journalist and kept his job past the first trial month.

Sarah was lonely at the weekends when he went home. She visited galleries or exhibitions – mentally noting the ones he might enjoy. She went alone to film previews, to the theatre. She walked in Kensington Gardens. She joined an aerobics class. She got through the interminable Sundays by reading all the newspapers and dozing all afternoon on the flat's tiny sunny balcony. She turned down invitations from men because they were not James, and because she thought it unfair to use them as stop gaps.

She often walked in Kensington Gardens and watched the children playing. One day a little boy stumbled and fell almost at her feet. She bent down and picked him up. He was warm and light. His body was chunky and compact. His legs were working like clockwork before she even replaced him on the ground. She set him upright and he staggered off, fired with determination. His mother smiled her thanks. Sarah smiled back but she was suddenly stricken with deep desire. She wanted a child of her own.

The If game changed – it became a threat. 'If you had a child we would have to give up the flat,' James said. 'If you had a child you would have to give up work.'

The leaves in the park started falling. The children were bulky parcels, wrapped in bright anoraks and duffle coats. Their faces were bright as holly berries in the cold air. Sarah longed to wrap up her own child warmly. 'If you had a child it would ruin your career,' James warned.

Sarah's weekends became bleak. She joined a gym and sweated on a training bench every Saturday afternoon. She grew fit and tightly muscled without pleasure. Her breasts were small and neat, dry. Her stomach was flat, her womb empty. She started to hate the waste of her monthly flow of blood. Next year she would be thirty-four.

The If Game

◆

'If I don't have a child soon it will be too late,' she said.

Christmas was the worst day of her life. James telephoned her on Christmas Day from the call box at the end of his road while walking with the twins on their new bikes. 'If I could be with you I would.'

She could hear them calling to him. He had arranged for flowers to be delivered and a bottle of champagne. He had left her a present, gift-wrapped under their tiny plastic tree. Sarah stayed in bed all Christmas Day, willing the time to pass.

It was after Christmas, during a flurry of cold weather, that she started to drop her contraceptive pills, one a night, carefully down the toilet. When the weather warmed and the croci flowered in great golden slushy pools under the dripping trees of the park, she knew she was pregnant. The If game changed again – becoming a game of bluff.

'If I left Miriam she would die,' James said. 'If I left my family the twins would be damaged.'

Sarah was sick in the mornings but she walked to work across the park and smiled at women with prams.

James was warned at the studio that his work was not good enough. One of the twins had a bout of food poisoning and James took a week's holiday and went home to help Miriam.

'If you won't have a termination, I don't know how we can go on,' he said before he went. 'We can't spoil our lives for an accident.'

Sarah bought two new larger bras and a couple of baggy

tops. She spoke to her boss about freelance shifts and found a small house at the unfashionable end of Hackney. She found a lodger who would help with the baby in return for cheap rent.

James missed a major story on his first day back and said he was sick of the pressures of national news.

'If I went back to Bristol I could walk into the evening news presenter job,' he said. 'I've got experience of a national newsroom now.'

'You mean to leave me and go back to Miriam,' Sarah said, stating the obvious.

'Oh no,' James said. The If game in its final phase was one of empty promises. 'If I worked in Bristol it would make no difference to us. If I lived at home again it would change nothing between us.'

In the autumn he transferred back to his old studio and went home to Miriam and the twins. Miriam greeted his return without excitement. She was remote from him, a cool woman. James found his interest stimulated by her indifference. She was not like his wife, she was like a stranger.

He bought her little gifts, bottles of wine, and small bouquets of flowers. She accepted them calmly, in the same way that she received squashy papier mâché models from the twins' art classes.

James telephoned Sarah every morning from the studio and visited her once a week. She was growing large with her pregnancy, she was often tired. Her little house's roof leaked, she had noisy neighbours. Sometimes she refused to make love. James caught the train home with relief. Now the twins were older they were in bed by eight and the evenings were quiet and ordered. Miriam cooked dinner for him and they listened to classical music. Miriam was going back to work as a graphic designer. James watched her growing independence with fascination.

'If you were my mistress,' he started. Miriam was sitting opposite him, there were candles on the table and the sweet honeyed smell of roasting chicken. Miriam was wearing a flowing kaftan and underneath, he thought, perhaps nothing. She looked more like a mistress than a wife. James felt the old, irresistible urge to play, to beguile, to seduce. 'If you were my mistress . . .'

Miriam smiled her confident wife's smile. She knew him very, very well. 'Oh no,' she said firmly, shaking her head. 'I should never be such a fool as that.'

The Conjuring Trick

First the cars: Gary drove a BMW, which was a perk of his
job with the finance company. Stella drove her own Metro,
she worked with a public relations company. She had
bought it herself – £800 down and repayments over five
years. Now the pensions: Gary had a complicated scheme
set up by a syndicate at work. When he received a large
bonus he transferred half of it straight into the pension
fund. Stella had a personal equity plan which deducted £100
every month from her account.

Their speech was full of movement and geography.
Stella's savings were solid as a rock but Gary's could go
through the roof. They spoke of ideas that would run and
run, a difficulty was being stuck between a rock and a hard
place. Their imagery was that of pioneers, facing adventure
and hardship. The excitement in their language concealed
the fact that he was a dealer in the city, and she wrote
advertising copy. They were completely impregnated with
the values of the 1980s, they thought that growth – indeed
excess – was never ending.

They had met at a dinner party and each had seen in the other the same sharp acquisitive bright face, like the one which smiled out of their own mirror every morning. Other people commented on the resemblance too, and when they were courting – which was hurried but exciting – they dressed alike to enhance the resemblance. They chose their clothes together, in shops like Gap and Principles and Next – shops which served and confirmed their taste of what was, and what was not, attractive. They paid with credit cards, and let the debts mount up.

They married in the spring of 1987 and bought their house a year later. Gary's reputation for astute business practice and Stella's flair were demonstrated in their choice. It was a big tumbling-down vicarage in the town centre, surrounded by a large derelict garden and a high red-brick wall. They had offered, and withdrawn their offer, produced a damning survey, put in a spoiler bid, and finally beaten the vendors (the Church of England at its least triumphant) down to a minimum price. Even so they were forced to cash in their pensions to pay the deposit, obtain a maximum mortgage, and top up the loan from a finance company. When they finally opened a bottle of champagne, surrounded by packing cases in the large echoing drawing room, they owed a breathtaking sum.

It didn't seem to matter, there was always more credit. They ripped out the old kitchen, including the working coal range, and put in slim tall units: slate grey with smoked glass. They took out a loan with another company to pay

for the central heating. They re-tiled the roof, they under-
pinned the walls, they put in a damp course. They carpeted
throughout, they curtained the tall draughty windows. Carpets and curtains were all grey or white, all the furniture
was a uniform matte black. At the end of 1989 the house
was worth four times the purchase price. If they had sold
then, they would have shown a profit of more than
£200,000.

'We'll hold on,' Gary said. There was no need for them
to sell. Gary's commission was rising and keeping pace with
the loan payments, Stella's job was secure and her prospects
of promotion were good. They took out a loan secured
against the new value of the house and went on holiday
to the Caribbean. They loved the place so much that they
bought a time-share apartment, a small deposit and the rest
to pay over ten years. They offered the house as security on
the loan. 'You've got to keep your capital liquid,' Gary said,
who understood about these things.

And then the world slumped and all the rules, all the
scenery was different, even the language was different.
People no longer spoke like pioneers, they talked like
defeated soldiers of retrenching, and pulling back, of managed failure and cutting losses. Gary was 'let go' – but he
had nowhere to go. They took away his car, and the new
double garage with the electric door stood half empty. They
made Stella redundant and then re-employed her as a freelance. She had to work from home, and pay her own tax
and expenses. She did not dare to complain.

They went to see the bank who no longer agreed with Gary that capital should be liquid. The thinking in the 1990s was that capital should be secure. They defaulted on the timeshare deal and lost all the money they had put in. Some of the goods they had purchased on loan agreements they could send back. But the expensive curtains and carpets, the luxury kitchen and the studio bathroom were fitted to the house, and could not be reclaimed or returned.

'We'll sell the house,' Gary decided. 'Recoup.'

But it was not easy to sell. Large houses were coming on the market almost every day. The price they had paid in the booming eighties had been a triumph – a steal. But they had poured money into the improvements and décor. Now people no longer wanted cold empty rooms, they wanted the country look. Potential buyers saw the elegant laboratory-like kitchen and wanted stencilled wood, and Agas. They had to put the house on the market for less than it had cost them, for less than it was worth. In any case they would see none of the money. It would go straight to the mortgage companies and then to the loan companies and to the bank. Gary had seen whole corporations go bankrupt, wiped off the flickering computer screen. He had never thought that his life and his house, and perhaps even his marriage, could be erased by a blinking green cursor into total blackness.

It was then, in their long evenings of desperate calculations and arguments and bitter regrets, that Gary thought of the ghost. He had read an article about a family who had suffered from a poltergeist, which threw chairs, smashed mirrors, broke glasses. One of the glossy magazines had paid them £50,000 for their story with pictures. 'It would pull us clear,' Gary said. 'Get us liquid.'

Stella knew how to contact newspapers, how to set up a story, who would buy. Gary set himself to fabricating evidence of a murder so foul that it would give rise to a gruesome – and therefore profitable – haunting.

'Children,' he said. 'It has to be children.'

Stella said nothing. She was working on the copy for an advertisement. She glanced up at him and did not try to hide the irritation in her face. 'Just do it,' she said. 'If you're so sure. And I can sell the story. But don't keep interrupting me. This has to be in by tomorrow.'

'Sorry,' he said. He was humble these days. He felt he owed her, just as he owed the bank, and the building society, and the loan companies, and the timeshare company. He owed them all.

He went to the library to research and then he struck lucky. There had been a murder, a particularly nasty murder, of three small children in a house in their street, way back in 1923. The local newspaper did not give the number of the house and Gary was certain that no-one would remember or, if they did, by then the story would be published and the cheque banked.

He copied down the details. The man, shell-shocked from the trenches, not knowing where he was, had come home from the pub, drunk and angry. The children had been locked in an upstairs room. He had staggered up the stairs and kicked in the door. He had no weapon, he had used his hands, his boots, and in the end his teeth. Even Gary, who was not a squeamish man, battled with nausea as he copied the details into his little notebook. They had called the man the Savage of Steel Crescent, an animal, a monster.

He brought the story home and Stella read it. 'Yes,' she said. 'I can sell this.'

Gary started work on the house. He treated the walls of the spare bedroom so that stains like blood seemed to be seeping through the subtle cream paper. Together they opened a couple of air vents, hidden in the cupboard, so the room was several degrees colder than the rest of the house. They practised their accounts of hearing the footsteps on the stairs, the cries for help. Stella was particularly good in her description of the creak on the floorboards of a heavy foot, the noise of the man stumbling, and then the heavy crash as he broke into the bedroom where the children were crying in fear.

They frightened themselves thoroughly with a complete dress rehearsal. 'It's perfect,' Gary said. 'Tomorrow you ring the papers. It's irresistible.'

They went to bed but Stella could not sleep. She felt afraid, her account of the murders had been too vivid, her heart still thudded as she thought of what she had described, so certainly, with such conviction. 'I suppose it is all right to do,' she said. 'It *is* lying.'

Gary had the answer. 'It's conjuring,' he said. 'Like stage

magic, like Paul Daniels. Now you see it, now you don't. Nobody asks: is it true?'

'No,' she said. But that night she dreamed that she heard a footstep and the strange monstrous snuffle of the man coming up the stairs, dead drunk on his hands and knees, inspired by a savage madness.

'You'll do it better if you're really scared,' Gary said in the morning. He was pale himself, with excitement. 'Call the newsdesks.'

They auctioned the story: there were three papers involved at the end, and the last one took the bid up to £80,000. That night Gary bought a bottle of champagne, they had almost forgotten the taste. Next day he signed the sale contract on the house with the buyer. They would clear their debts. They might even show a profit of a couple of thousand pounds. They could rent a little flat, take their furniture, and start again. They were young, no slump lasts forever, Gary would get work, they would rebuild their lives.

The reporter and the photographer came together, half an hour before they were due. Stella and Gary, wise in such methods, had been ready for the previous hour. They showed the room with the little bloodstained handprints on the wall, at the pitiful low level. They showed the layer upon layer of wallpaper that they had put on to cover the stains, and to cover them again. The reporter shivered at the icy chill of the room. 'This is really spooky,' she said.

But the strongest moment was when Stella, in the

kitchen, her eyes wide with real fear, said that she heard the man coming upstairs on his hands and knees, sniffing like a dog, up to the bedroom door, and sniff, sniff, sniff on the threshold, and then his roar as he flung himself up and against it.

'I hear the children cry out – and then I hear a dreadful thing . . .'

'What?'

Stella went pale. 'I hear the murder,' she said. 'I hear a crack, a bone breaking, I hear a little scream, a helpless scream, and then I hear an awful sound . . . an awful sound . . .'

She broke off, she could hardly breathe.

'What sound?' the reporter pressed her. Gary covered Stella's hand with his own and felt that she was icy cold.

'Steady on . . .' he said softly.

'I hear him biting,' she said. 'Biting like a dog. A terrible grunt and snap and gobbling sound.' She put her hands over her face. 'I know it's him,' she whispered. 'Biting into the baby's throat, and chest, and little stomach.'

They took photographs: of the bedroom, of the stairs, of Gary and Stella arm-in-arm at the front door. Stella refused to go into the room itself – a nice touch, Gary thought – but then he saw her white face and thought that she was near to convincing herself. The reporter had brought the cheque. As soon as she were gone he banked it and paid for a rush transfer. They had £80,000 in their account at the close of business, they were in the clear.

When he got home Stella was having a bath, the door firmly locked. He glanced into the haunted bedroom. In the twilight the little handprints seemed darker, and there seemed more of them. He shook his head. He was spooked by the story, by Stella's convincing acting, by the horror of the whole fiction.

He tapped on the bathroom door, and heard her little scream of fright at the sudden noise, quickly repressed. 'Come down for a drink!' he called.

She did not come down. He sat in the kitchen and drank a couple of glasses of brandy. When he went up to bed she was pretending to be asleep and would not speak to him. Gary climbed into bed beside her, stubbornly clinging to his sense of relief that they had pulled a clever scam, a brilliant sting. Their conjuring trick, their once-in-a-lifetime conjuring trick, had saved them.

He fell asleep. Stella turned on her back, and lay wakeful in the half darkness of the room. And then she heard him. She heard the front door quietly click open and the stumble as his foot found the first stair. She heard the treads creak, one slow creak after another, as he walked up, and then he fell to his hands and knees and crawled the last steps. She heard him at the spare bedroom door, and the dreadful snuffle snuffle, like a dog, like an ogre. But instead of going in to the empty room, instead of being fooled by the red paint and the trickery, there was a terrifying silence, a pause. And she sensed him, she could almost see him swinging his head from side to side, trying to catch a scent, to discover where he should go. As she lay frozen, trying not to move, holding her breath, she knew he was trying to catch *her* scent, listening for her. Then she heard a little grunt, of satisfaction, of recognition, and she heard the slow beast's crawl as he came remorselessly towards her door.

And she remembered then, as she should have remembered before, that there is another sense of the word conjuring as well as trickery and pretend magic. To conjure means to summons, to invoke, to call up.

They had conjured him.

The Wave Machine

◆

He hated the phone ringing in the early hours of the morning. It jerked him from sleep, and he liked his sleep. His first thought was that Tom, his brother, was worse. Tom had been ill all winter, one of those lingering mystery illnesses. He knew he should have cared more; Tom was his only brother. But he knew himself to be a selfish man: a bachelor, an artist. He did not care for anyone very much.

'Hello?' He could hear the caution in his own voice.

'It's Veronica,' she said sharply. 'I am sorry to wake you so early.' She didn't sound in the least sorry, he thought. She sounded demanding. 'It's an emergency.'

He stifled his groan and sat up in bed, rubbing his face with his hand, erasing the hangover, feeling the enjoyable rasp of stubble. 'What is it?'

'It's Tom,' she said, as he had known she would. 'They want to start a programme of allergy tests. I have to take him in every day for the next two months.'

'Oh.' He twitched back the curtain by his bed. Outside

◈

a perfect peach and pearl sky was reflected into a gently breathing sea.

'I need help,' she said, then specified: 'I need *your* help.'

He said nothing, hoping that his silence was discouraging.

'I can't cope with Katie,' she said. 'It's an hour's drive to the hospital, and then an hour's drive home again, every morning and every evening. She can't do four hours in the car every day.'

He thought for a moment. 'Shouldn't she be at school?'

'She is only just four,' she said. 'She doesn't start until September, and already she's dreading it.'

'Nursery?'

'Summer holidays.'

'Isn't there some kind of crèche?'

'Not one that stays open till nine o'clock at night,' she said.

He let the silence stretch. He knew that having a child at all had been Tom's idea. Veronica had never been more than a reluctant mother.

'It's too bad if it's not convenient,' she said brutally. 'I can't cope. You'll have to have her. It won't be for long. Just till she starts school in September.'

He thought of the long sun-warmed days that had spread before him. He had planned to start a new sculpture, something abstract and mechanical-looking, a wicked stone robot-thing. He did not want a little girl in his house, which was a spare clear environment. He did not want a little girl who would need food that he did not like, such as fish fingers and perhaps beefburgers. He emphatically did not want a little girl curtailing his visits to the local pub and chaperoning him when his lover – a fashion journalist – arrived unexpectedly, demanding an exotic welcome.

'Surely there must be agencies?' he asked vaguely, deliberately not knowing what he was suggesting.

'You want me to put her into care?'

'Oh, all right,' he said irritably. 'I'll have her. But you'll have to send me instructions. I won't have a clue.'

'There's nothing to do,' she assured him. 'Katie's no trouble.'

He did not believe her, until they arrived and the little girl carried her own small suitcase up the stairs. They left her to look around her room and the pretty view over the sea. As he poured Veronica a gin and tonic he heard little footsteps overhead.

'What's she doing?' he asked nervously, like a new owner with a strange pet.

'Unpacking I should think, she's madly tidy,' Veronica said. 'God knows where she gets it from.' She finished her drink and slapped down her glass. 'Must go.'

'Already?'

She nodded. 'I have to take Tom in to the clinic this evening. He sent his love.'

'Will she be upset when you leave?'

Veronica shook her head. 'She's a calm little thing. You'll

see. Any problem, ring me up. I'll come down at the weekend if I can.'

He did not want her to go, but he had no excuse to keep her. She called up the stairs to the little girl, and then kissed her in a businesslike fashion. 'Your Uncle Michael will look after you,' she said. 'Ask him for whatever you need.'

Michael looked at the small serious face between the jaunty bunches of brown hair and wondered what outrageous demands she might invent. She looked back with large trusting brown eyes and smiled a gap-toothed smile. 'I need to go to the sea,' she said.

'After lunch,' he said. 'We'll go after lunch.'

They waved goodbye to Veronica and then the little girl took his hand as they walked through the house to the kitchen.

'I'm going to have soup and a bread roll,' he said. 'Do you want fish fingers?'

'I'll be like you,' she decided.

'I usually read at lunch,' he said, defending his bachelor habits. 'I read the newspaper.'

'Oh, so do I,' she said, and went to her room and fetched a brightly coloured comic. They sat, rather solemnly, side by side spooning soup from matching bowls, reading their papers.

'We don't have a nice nap after lunch,' she asserted when she had finished her soup.

'Don't we?'

'Can we go to the sea?'

'Oh, all right,' he said. His cottage was at the top of a steep cliff path, delightful for visitors but wearisome for someone who lived there all the year round. In his first year he had trotted down to swim in the sea every sunny morning. In his second year he remembered the steep climb back up to his house and went less frequently. This summer, his third in the little house, he had not been down to the sea at all.

'Do I have to wear my boots?'

'I don't know!' he exclaimed.

'No, I don't,' she said decidedly.

He thought longingly of the afternoon he would have had without her, there was horse-racing on the television and he could have sketched and looked at the screen over the top of his sketchbook. But she was determined to be out, and the sunshine was warm and welcoming.

The beach was a revelation.

They hardly walked at all. As soon as she arrived on the rounded stones at the foot of the cliff path she thumped down on her red-trousered bottom and examined them, one after the other.

'Don't you want to walk down to the sea?' he asked, and encountered a glance which was so full of wonder that he felt humbled, as if in the presence of a miracle.

'They're all different!' she said.

'Yes.' He was about to say 'I know', when he realised with rare honesty that he did not know. He had scrunched over the stones hundreds of times, cursing their sharpness when he was barefoot, but he had never properly looked at them.

She held up for him a rounded pebble almost scarlet in colour and beside it a sea-smoothed white flint with a dark slaty heart, just visible through an entrancing little keyhole. 'Look!' she said.

He could not resist her interest. 'And here!' he said. He had found a pale speckled stone, oval-shaped.

'An egg!' she exclaimed.

'Let's put it in a nest,' he suggested.

'Oh yes!'

Together they amassed dark-coloured pebbles and formed them in a circle. Inside, they placed the first speckled stone and then hunted for others. In the end they found half a dozen and she arranged them very carefully, and then squatted solemnly on top of them. He could not think, at first, what she was doing.

'Hatching,' she said with dignity.

It seemed to him that she sat on her little nest for an extraordinarily long time. The heat went from the sun and an onshore breeze started up.

'I'm getting cold,' he said. 'Let's go.'

She rose up and started up the path willingly enough but after the first set of steps she was tired and wanted to rest. He had to urge her on the next set, and promise her all sorts of delights for tea to get her up the next set. They counted steps together for the final set and he reached the top with a sense of achievement.

He had planned an omelette for his tea and she agreed to share, but was reluctant to let him break the eggs. Feeling rather ridiculous he blew the eggs for her, with a pinprick in the shell at each end so that she had a complete box of empty egg shells. She took them up to her bath with her and floated them in the water.

'Do I stay up very late here?' she enquired.

'No,' he said decidedly. 'You go to bed and stay in your room.'

'But I look at my books in bed?'

'All right,' he said grudgingly. 'But you stay in your room.'

Her lower lip trembled slightly. 'Unless I am afraid of the dark,' she suggested.

For a moment he was terrified that she would cry. 'You are not afraid of the dark,' he said firmly. 'You can see in the dark because you're an owl. You were an owl on the beach all afternoon and owls can see perfectly well in the dark.'

'Oh,' she said, absorbing that information. She climbed into her bed and he tucked her in, feeling as if he were acting a part in some idealised nursery scene. She looked very angelic. When she raised her little face for a goodnight kiss she smelled of soap. He touched the soft petal of her cheek with his lips, feeling as if he were too old and self-indulgent to approach such pellucid innocence.

'Can we go to the sea again tomorrow?' she asked.

'We didn't get to the sea today,' he pointed out.

She smiled contentedly. 'Can we try again tomorrow?'

'All right.'

*   *   *

Downstairs, he poured himself a large Scotch with a splash of water. Normally he would drink half a bottle but tonight he thought he would have only one glass. There were things to put away: toys and her shoes, which were sandy. Her little socks were discarded on the stairs. To his surprise he did not resent the chores. He felt rather contented. He tidied up and then dropped into his chair and switched on the television. He had a warm sense of having a home, rather than merely somewhere to live. He had a little girl sleeping peacefully under his roof; a nestling in the stone nest.

The telephone rang. 'It's me,' said Zoë. 'I can come down on Friday night. I thought I'd take the train and you could meet me in Plymouth. I'll leave Sunday afternoon.'

'There's a complication,' he said.

'Oh?' She was instantly suspicious. 'What sort of complication?'

'My niece is staying with me for the summer. She's four.'

'Poor little sod,' she said rudely. 'Does she drink whisky?'

'She's fine,' he said. 'No trouble, and you're welcome to come. Take a taxi from the station, I can't get out to collect you.'

'I had a rather . . .' She dropped her voice into a husky drone which someone had once told her was seductive. '. . . I had a rather *adult* weekend in mind. Can't you farm her out for two days? Get her back when I've gone?'

He thought it odd that in one day his views had changed so completely. 'She's not a puppy, I can't put her in kennels,' he said abruptly. 'If you want to see me, you see her too. This is her home for the summer. I'm not throwing her out just because you've got a spare weekend.'

'Oh, screw you then!' she shouted and slammed down the phone.

He waited a moment and then quietly replaced the receiver. He sounded out his own mind for regret and found none. He took up his sketch pad and started to work on the sharp wicked robot face of his planned statue. Nothing came. Instead he doodled a set of attractively rounded and speckled pebbles.

Next day they set out for the sea again, and once again they were waylaid by the extraordinary variety of pebbles. This time they decided to amass all of the white pebbles on the beach and built them into a dangerously unstable pyramid. They played until sunset and then he lured her up the steps to the cottage, by counting them. It was an unsuccessful exercise since Katie could count no more than three. He taught her the numbers up to ten, and felt a pleasing sense of virtue.

It was more than a week before they exhausted the pleasures of the pebble strand and finally arrived at the sea's edge. The tide was high and Katie stood beside him solemnly watching the waves wash in and out. He knew her well enough now to see that something was puzzling her. After nearly half an hour of silent contemplation she turned to him:

◈

'Where's the machine?'

'Machine?' He was startled. He had been thinking of his proposed statue, which was not progressing at all. He had a plan for it now: pincer arms and a sharp dead face, but he could feel no enthusiasm for it. He would never start sculpting until he could feel powerfully that it was the right thing, the only thing to do. This time the surge of energy was slow in coming. He wondered if the even routine of Katie's days were sapping his spontaneity. He wondered if he were becoming boring: a child-bound housewife.

'Where's the machine?' she repeated. 'The wave machine.'

For a moment he could not think what she meant and then he laughed aloud. She had been brought up in a town, she had only ever seen waves made in a swimming pool with a wave machine. She was too small to understood that the machine was trying to reproduce the real movement of the sea. She had mistaken the mechanical copy for the real thing. When she met the reality – the gently shushing waves of the calm sea – she looked for a synthetic explanation.

'There isn't a machine,' he said, smiling. 'The sea moves like this all on its own.'

She had a delightful chuckle. Her eyes narrowed and her smile, with the endearing gap at the top teeth, widened. 'Silly Mike,' she said confidently. 'Of course there's a machine. I'll find it for you.'

She took him by the hand and pulled him to his feet and

they set off along the beach looking at the red stone cliffs and under the larger pebbles, inspecting cave entrances and rock pools. 'It's somewhere here,' she said certainly. 'It's got to be. To make the waves.'

For the rest of that summer that was her project. They still collected stones, and when the tide was so low that the small sandbar was exposed they built ornate and beautiful sand castles. He enjoyed working with sand so much that he started to puzzle out a way of using it in his art. But every day Katie searched for the machine which made the waves.

The phone call, at the end of August, came as a shock. 'Tom's coming out at the weekend,' Veronica said. 'They think it was a virus, after all, not an allergy. He's miles better anyway, thank God. I'll collect her tomorrow.'

Dismay clutched at him. 'No hurry.'

'Darling, she has to start school!'

'I forgot.'

'You can have her again in the holidays, if it's been such a success,' she offered sarcastically.

He thought for a moment. 'D'you know, I would like that.'

Veronica laughed. 'Who'd have thought it?'

They took a last ceremonial walk on the beach together.

'You don't mind going to school, do you, Katie?' he asked anxiously.

'Oh no,' she said confidently. 'Not now I can count.'

She slipped her hand from his grasp and ran ahead. It had been a high tide in the night and there were new and interesting beachcombings. He gathered up driftwood as he walked behind her; the driftwood, the pebbles, the fluid complex movements of sand sculpture – he could not think how he had missed it before.

'Mike!' she suddenly screamed. 'Mike!'

His heart missed a horror-struck beat. 'Katie!' he yelled and raced towards her.

She was dancing with excitement. Half-embedded in the sand, with rust spotting the chrome, was the thrown-away grille of a car radiator.

'Here it is! Here it is!' she shrieked.

For a moment he could not think what she meant and then he realised that it did indeed look very like the vents for a wave machine set into the edge of the sea.

'To make the waves! To make the waves!' she crowed. 'I knew it was here!'

He crouched down beside her so that her bright eyes were level with his own. 'But isn't it rather small, Katie? To move the whole sea? To shift the whole of the ocean?'

She shook her head solemnly. 'Something doesn't have to be very big to make a lot of difference,' she said.

'Oh, Katie,' he said lovingly. 'That's very true.'

The Magic Box

◆

I awoke in the half-light of morning, a moody monochrome as if it had been carefully lit by an expert. I raised myself on one arm and looked at Mark fast asleep, his perfect profile, his tousled hair. The bed dipped beneath my pregnant heaviness and he stirred and said something in his sleep. I felt a moment of utter dread, in case it was her name, in case he was dreaming of her. I froze, hardly daring to breathe, in that painful tension which I had learned in the past hard year when he had told me that he loved her, and that he would leave me.

He had not gone. I had won. I screamed and then cried – great floods of tears that poured from my rage and my hurt. I barricaded myself in my studio and smashed up my equipment: my precious lights, my screens, my cameras. I swung a tripod like an axe in an orgy of destruction to show him, in a shower of glass, metal, and paper, that I needed him even more than I needed the tools of my trade. That I needed him more than I needed my profession, more than my lifestyle. More than my life itself.

He was stony-faced, a cupid in marble, while I wept and begged, and then he went to her. She was as peaceful as a weekday church. The more I raged, the more quietly emphatic was the calm she wove around him. He told me that she grieved for the pain I was suffering. He told me that he had seen her weep for me. I pictured the two of them, their faces very close at a candle-lit table, saying softly what a shame it was I could not accept that his love for me had ended; what a shame it was that I was so blind not to see that he had to move on.

I would not accept it. He had given me no warning, nothing had changed between us. We made love, we planned to move house, we wanted a baby, we went out to work during the week and we lazed around together at weekends. How was I supposed to know that he had changed? I didn't believe he *had* changed. What I thought then, and still believe now, was that she gave him the idea that he could do better.

She made him think that he could do better than marriage with me. She is rich. She has a beautiful flat by the river. She set aside a room for him to write in and called it his study. She ordered her Filipino housekeeper to take him coffee and make him small delicious lunches. She never let anyone touch his papers. She told him that she wanted to nurture his talent. She told him he should give up his job editing the magazine, that she would keep him while he wrote. She told him he was a great writer and he should not be troubled with a boring little job and an hysterical wife.

He didn't return for my passion, nor for my anger, nor for my grief. I telephoned him one night, the final night, at her flat, and told him that I consented. That I surrendered. That I would let him go, if he would let me go. I offered him his release and my release in those words. I meant him to wonder what I meant by 'let me go'.

He didn't pause to think. I heard the relief in his voice. Eight miles across London I sensed her secret triumph. I went to the bathroom and took one of his old razor blades and washed it carefully – as if I should fear blood poisoning! – then stretched my hands into the bath. I drew a smooth line along the blue vein on one wrist, and then on the other.

It didn't hurt. The skin opened, I could see a pinker layer beneath it, opening like a zip fastener. I could see the blue membrane of the vein sliced as neat as the stem of a violet. Then the blood welled up in copious warmth out of my wrists and down into my cupped hands, and overflowed into the bath. I watched it, smiling. Even when the pain started and my tears dripped off my cheeks into the bath, I was still smiling.

It was Maggie who broke down the door. She phoned the ambulance, remembered my blood group for an emergency transfusion. It was Maggie who went around to Helen's flat and leaned on the doorbell until Helen's voice spoke sharply over the intercom. It was Maggie who kept her finger on the bell until Mark came. It was Maggie who threw him in her car and drove him to the hospital where he saw me, drugged into smiling calm, limp in bed. It was Maggie who cursed him with all the richness of her backstreet childhood language, and Maggie who forced him into tears and into the weeping confession that he didn't know what he was doing. That he didn't know which of us he wanted.

When I came out of hospital he was at home. He never told me how he had parted from Helen and I never found again the bold courage of a confident lover which would have allowed me to ask. Since that day, as the aching scars on my wrists slowly healed, as we sold the town house, and bought a lovely old ramshackle vicarage in the Cotswolds, as I conceived our child, I never found again the careless certainty that I had known before Helen.

I lay back in bed and watched the light brighten on the ceiling. I didn't wake Mark. It was a Saturday and he could sleep until noon if he wished, then we were going to a furniture auction at a country house. Our things were spread very thin in this rambling house, a six-bedroomed vicarage, and besides, I wanted old furniture around me. I wanted to give Mark a walnut-wood desk with one of those slatted rolling lids, and a special room where he could write. I wanted a rocking cradle and one of those high old fire guards with the padded tops for the nursery. I wanted to create a house that looked as if we had lived there forever. A house that no man would leave.

I was disappointed by the sale. I had a romantic idea of an auction at a country house, but much of the furniture had been bought in and most of it was frankly shabby. The nice pieces were snapped up by dealers at prices that we couldn't afford. Mark and I watched the bidding, and then wandered outside to where they were serving teas on the terrace. There was a table, on the corner of the terrace, piled high with junk: chipped china, bent silver-plate trays, some stained and rather smelly shawls ... and a most beautiful rosewood box.

I recognised it at once. It was a carrying case for one of the earliest cameras. Lying beside it was a long matching chest. I bent down awkwardly, allowing for the bulge at my waist, and clicked back the brass clips. It was lined inside with red plush velvet, motheaten and worn now. In the lid, the craftsman – a scientific instrument maker from Glasgow – had engraved his name. Inside were stacked thick pieces of glass.

'What are they?' Mark asked casually.

'Glass photographic plates,' I whispered in awe. 'And this should be ...' I opened the lid of the nearby case. Gleaming on the padded cushions was the heavy wooden box of an old camera with the leathery snout of the bellows compressed into a velvet pocket beside it.

'It's lovely,' I said. 'Help me get it out!'

Mark glanced around, hesitated. 'Come on, Mark!' I said. 'It's for sale. I want to see it.'

He shrugged and helped me drag the box from under the table. It was deliciously heavy, with the weight of solid wood and hand-turned brass.

The black hood for the cameraman was packed in one of the pockets, the black metal slide and glass plate were in the back of the camera, ready for use. I touched the wood of the top of the camera, and gently twisted the focus puller. The lens cap on the front was made of wood. It came off with a gentle half-turn.

'I see you're interested in the camera,' said a voice behind me. I straightened up awkwardly. He was a man in his fifties, his cheeks crimsoned with broken veins, and a nose to match. 'Belonged to my grandfather. He took the pictures. The plates are in the other box.'

'It's beautiful,' I said. 'What was his name?'

'Clive Cozens,' the man said. He put out his hand. 'I'm George Cozens.'

I smiled. 'I'm Clare Banford,' I said. 'This is my husband, Mark.'

George Cozens narrowed his eyes. 'Clare Banford the photographer?' he asked.

I nodded. I was surprised he knew my name. I specialise in nature photography, especially birds and rare plants. Not many people see my pictures, even fewer remember the names of photographers.

'I've got a first edition of Hall which you illustrated,' he said. 'Bought it for the pictures alone.'

I beamed at him. 'Thank you,' I said.

'You still working?' he demanded with a glance at my maternity smock and the swelling curve underneath.

'No,' I said. 'Actually I've sold my studio in London.

We've moved out to Clayhall Rectory, just near here. But I'll get back to work again as soon as the baby's born.'

He nodded.

'Is this for sale?' I asked, gesturing to the camera, gleaming in its nest of velvet.

'Are you interested?' he asked.

I heard Mark give a little 'ttssk' of indignation.

'I don't have a lot of money to spend,' I said cautiously. 'We were supposed to be buying furniture.'

George Cozens nodded. 'Would you use it?' he asked. 'Or just keep it?'

'I'd use it,' I said honestly. 'I'm going to set up my own darkroom at home, and I've been experimenting with older equipment. It's not often you get the glass plates with the camera like this.'

'And they're developed,' he said. He bent down and pulled out one of the thick glass plates. 'See?'

Very faintly I could just make out the shape of some tribesman. He was half-naked, his body painted, feathers in his hair, beads slung around his neck and waist. He carried a spear and glared at the camera.

'My God,' I said wonderingly. 'How old is this?'

'Taken in 1890,' George Cozens said. 'My grandfather's last expedition. He went up the Orinoco and took pictures of everything that he could make stand still for long enough! It's a vanished world. The rain forest before white men came. The tribes. All dead now. All gone.'

'He took pictures of people?'

'Not many,' he said. He slid the glass back into its padded slot. 'Most of them thought it would steal their souls and refused. They called it the magic box. That chappie must have been a plucky one,' he chuckled.

'Look here,' he continued with sudden generosity. 'You can have this. It was given to my grandfather as a gift by an established Scots photographer. I'd like to hand it on. I'll ask you for one favour.'

I gaped in astonishment. 'Anything!'

'If you get some pictures from it, print me a spare copy and let me have it, signed by you. I'll have a Banford collection. Might frame them.'

I put my hand out. 'It's a deal,' I said. 'And I promise also I'll not sell it. If I can't make it work, I'll let you have it back.'

He took my hand in his. 'Good,' he said. 'It's yours.'

Mark grumbled when I set up a darkroom even before we had finished painting the nursery.

'I want to take pictures of the baby with the camera,' I said. 'And I can't wait to get a good look at these glass plates.'

We sat before the fire that evening, opened the box and took them out and wiped them clean together. There were some amazing pictures of deep tropical forest and a deep sepia brown river winding beneath tree trunks as high as the towers of a cathedral. There were a few shots of birds – rather disappointing, I thought. One was obviously dead, and one had flown before the exposure was completed. There were lots of photographs of the Indian villages from long distance, but very few people. The picture I had first seen, of the man with the spear and the bold stare, was the best. In one of the others the sitter had obviously lost his courage and fled before ten seconds.

I printed them all as a record, and sent prints to George Cozens. There were two plates which were blank so I cleaned them and treated them for my own use. That would give me one in the camera and one to spare until I got some more glass.

'It'll drive you mad,' Mark said with satisfaction. He knew how much film I liked to use before I had even one worthwhile shot. 'You'll never manage with only two shots at any picture.'

'It'll be good discipline for me,' I said, smiling. The baby shifted inside me, and I took Mark's hand and laid it on my rounded belly so he could feel the movement.

'D'you feel her?' I asked. 'Can you feel her kick?'

Mark nodded. 'I need to make a phone call,' he said. 'You go on up to bed, you must be tired.'

I went slowly upstairs. Behind me the sitting room door closed gently. I heard the click of the phone as he picked it up. I didn't know who he was phoning. I held to the bannister and took a deep shuddering breath. The scars on my wrists tightened in remembered pain. I wondered if I had the courage to go back downstairs and open the door which he had shut so quietly. I wondered if I had the

courage to say simply and honestly to him: 'Mark, you
made a decision. You came home to me, we moved house,
I gave up my work and we are having a child. These are
not decisions you can play with. I am not a hobby you can
take up, or put down. You must not see her, or phone her,
or even think of her again.'

I waited on the stairs. I heard his voice say something, and
then silence as the other person replied. I knew I could not
find the courage to make demands of Mark. I was a hostage
to fear. And besides, I said to myself, as I turned and went
up the stairs, I might be lucky: it might not be Helen on the
other end of that low-voiced conversation at all.

The pains started that night as we slept. They woke me,
like a nudge in the belly. For a little while I lay on my
back and smiled at the moonlit ceiling, thinking of my
baby, on her way to be born at last, after these long months
of waiting. I felt myself to be blessed, blessed beyond and
above anything I could ever have earned. Mark had come
back to me, we now lived where the air was so sweet that
you could taste it on your tongue, and my baby, who would
make us a family, an indissoluble unit, was coming in this
moonlit quiet night.

I rolled over so I could see the clock. I watched the hands
move and timed the uncontrollable clenching of my body.
I breathed lightly, as I had learned to do, and then I woke
Mark. He leaped out of bed in a panic, like a film version
of an anxious father. He dragged on a track suit, he
stumbled over my case at the door. He thrust clothes at

me, imploring me to hurry. He slapped his forehead when he remembered that the car was low on petrol after our trip to the sale. I smiled. I felt as if I were floating, out to sea a long long way. As if I too, like my baby, was starting on a journey to an unknown country. By this time tomorrow night, I would hold my child in my arms.

I was not afraid. Not at any time, though the labour lasted through the night and the baby was not born until half past ten in the morning. I was deeply tired then and I slept. The last thing I saw before I slept was Mark turning out his pockets for change for the telephone to tell people that our baby had been born, and that she was a perfect brown-headed blue-eyed girl. 'Not Helen,' I thought as I slid into sleep. I didn't want to say it. I trusted him. He would not, I knew he would not, telephone Helen to tell her our child was born. Not right away.

I hated the hospital. The cheerful insouciance of the nurses who changed my baby's nappy with lightning skill, and wrapped her so she stopped crying, could not endear it to me. I came out after two days. My doctor said I was well; and anyway Maggie, my friend, had promised to come and stay and look after us all.

She and Mark had a silent truce. He had not liked himself that night, when she had dragged him away from Helen. Now they were either side of my bed again and he remembered that she had rescued him from a fantasy of selfishness. He didn't like looking bad in front of anyone. Especially not women. Maggie was matter-of-fact.

'I bet you're glad now, Mark,' was all she ever said. She picked my little girl, Penelope, out of her hospital perspex cot and hugged her close. 'I bet you're happy now.'

Mark looked happy. He could not do enough for me, for Penny. He took a fortnight off work and he got up through the night, and dozed in a chair during the day. He looked exhausted, but he glowed from inside. Maggie nodded at me and smiled with shared knowledge that she, and I, and even little Penelope, had won.

As soon as I felt halfway back to normal I brought out the camera and showed it to Maggie. We waited until the baby was asleep. I didn't want her face blurred by moving during the exposure. Maggie and I set up the camera while Mark was out shopping. It took a lot of doing. I used a modern tripod to get the angle right. I didn't think that amounted to serious cheating. I plunged under the hood at the back and gazed at my baby through the thick glass window. Then I slid in the treated glass, took off the lens cap, pulled out the shielding slide and counted, slowly in my head, up to twenty-five.

'Why twenty-five?' Maggie asked.

'It's my age,' I said. 'It's as good as any other figure. I haven't a clue how long I should leave it.'

We did two shots, with my two glass plates, and then I took them away to my darkroom and printed them up at once. I used sepia colours, a sentimental gesture to old Clive Cozens, the photographer who followed the fashion of his time and preferred sepia. Penny looked delicate, ethereal in the light brown. I loved the effect. I did two copies for me, one for George Cozens as I had promised, and one for Maggie.

When Mark came home he brought steak for dinner – and a polaroid camera. 'If we have to wait for photographs that satisfy you, we'll be celebrating her wedding,' he said, and kissed me on the top of my head.

We drank a good bottle of wine between the three of us and then we went to bed. Penelope was asleep in the cradle at the bottom of our bed. I kissed her gently but she didn't stir so I thought I would leave her to sleep.

She did not wake me for feeding in the middle of the night.

She did not wake at all.

When I woke in the morning, to that dreadful silence, with a clutch of unknown terror like a cold fist grabbing my belly, I knew it had happened to her, to us. She was cold in her little crib. And the only thing I had left of her was the limp tiny body, and the pictures in the darkroom.

Maggie stayed with us. Through the speechless agony of the next few days, Maggie took the phone calls, made the arrangements, ordered the flowers. Maggie chose the little white coffin and the white marble headstone. I could not bear to think of them. Mark and I fell into depths of complete silence and avoidance. He slept in another room while I tossed and turned in our bed. I kept starting up in the night, thinking I heard her crying for me. The ache in my wrists matched the raw gulf inside me.

Maggie stayed. A full month. It was summer holiday at the school where she taught, and she cancelled her trip to America to stay with me until I could get through the day without weeping. She stayed until Mark was writing again, until we were eating ordinary meals and digging the garden, and talking about a conservatory. Then one day I came in from shopping, and the camera, the beautiful rosewood camera, was up on the tripod and Maggie was settling herself in front of it.

'Take my picture,' she said. 'I fancy myself in a sepia print.'

I knew why she was doing it. Maggie is clever but transparent. Mark was back to his work, editing his literary magazine, writing his novel. I should be back to work too. And in a little while, we would have another child. But he or she would always be my second child.

'Take my picture,' Maggie said again, beaming at the camera. 'Go on.'

I dumped the shopping down on the table and I was going to refuse, but the rosewood camera was warm under my fingertips, and the brass knobs on the leather bellows were dulled and dusty. I pulled a Kleenex out of my pocket and wiped them without thinking. Then I dived under the cape, took off the lens cap and saw the oddly upside-down image of Maggie, sitting on her head by the open window and the honeysuckle framing her.

'It's good,' I said reluctantly. 'Bit chocolate-boxy.'

I went to my dark room. The two glass plates were

cleaned and treated, ready for use. Safe under the red light where I had stacked them after I had printed my two pictures of Penny. Clear and clean as if she had never been there at all. As clear as a stream after someone has crossed it, and gone on.

I took them gently and wiped them lovingly, then I clipped one into the metal shield and took it through to the kitchen where Maggie sat smiling in the sunshine.

I slid it into the camera, and pulled out the shield. I counted carefully. 'Why only ten?' asked Maggie.

'Brighter light,' I said briefly. We both remembered the cool shade as Penny had slept.

I put the lens cap on, slid in the metal shield, and carried the plate to my darkroom. The picture was a good one. Maggie sat like some loving guardian angel in the window-seat of my kitchen, with the sunlight behind her, and the honeysuckle flowers like little trumpets around her solid silhouette.

'I look fat,' she said indignantly when I brought out her copy.

'You look real,' I replied. Then while she prepared lunch I drifted back into my darkroom and printed the other copies. One for me. One for George Cozens.

The picture, 'Maggie and honeysuckle', was a farewell gift. That evening she leaned forward with her chin on her hands and smiled impartially at both of us. 'I'm leaving you two chickabiddies, I need to go home.'

Mark looked blank. 'I'm so used to having you here, I

had forgotten you had a home,' he said. 'D'you have to go, Maggie?'

'Yes,' she said. She reached a hand out and touched his arm. 'I'm glad I've not outstayed my welcome. But term starts next week and I want to get home. I've got to prepare some work, and my house and garden have been neglected too long. I'm not far away, remember.'

I felt my throat tighten and tears at the back of my eyes. 'I'm glad you were here, Maggie,' I said. My voice was quavery. 'I don't think we would have survived this without you.'

Maggie shot a quick look at Mark to see if he was going to reach out to me. When he didn't move she came around the table and hugged me. 'You'd have made it through,' she said gently. 'You're a survivor, you are. You don't know how strong you are.'

We opened another bottle of wine and we drank it in the sitting room, lighting the fire of applewood and pine cones more for the light than for the warmth. I watched the shadows flicker on the wall and saw Mark's beloved face lit in profile by the warm glow of wood embers.

'I'm going to start doing portraits,' I said suddenly. 'It's time I got back to work. I shall try portraits for a change.'

Maggie beamed at me. 'And I'll be in an exhibition,' she said. 'Fame at last.'

It was two before we went upstairs to bed, and that night Mark didn't sleep in the spare room. He came to my bed and we made love slowly, with great care as if either of us might shatter with sorrow. When he slept he turned away from me. And when I woke in the morning he was gone.

Maggie and I ate a leisurely breakfast and then she went upstairs to pack her case. I lent her some books, and she took some flowers from the garden. I took a cutting of the honeysuckle and embedded it into a pot for transplanting into her London windowbox.

When the time came for her to leave she held me very tightly. 'You are a survivor,' she said again. 'I meant what I said last night. You are a survivor.'

I tipped my head back so that I could see her face. 'There are some things I'd rather not survive,' I said. 'This past year – Mark leaving me, and then Penny's death – I'd rather never have known those pains.'

Maggie smiled. She looked very old and wise. 'You learn from them,' she said gently. 'One day you will be able to see them for what they are. Penny's death is a tragedy, but Mark leaving you, in truth, was little more than inconvenient.'

I jerked back at that. 'Inconvenient!' I said.

She smiled. 'You always have a picture in your head,' she said gently. 'That's what makes you such a good photographer. You always have a picture in your head of how you want things to look. You liked the look of you and Mark together, and so you did everything you could to get and to hold that picture. But it's only a pretty picture, it's not real. The real Mark is not how you see him at all.'

I stepped back from her. I was speechless. She gave me

a mischievous wink. 'Oh, don't get all cross,' she said. She slung her handbag in her car, slipped behind the wheel and slammed the door. She wound down the window and smiled at me. 'Chocolate boxes,' she said. 'Chocolate box pictures.' Then she backed the car carefully around, and drove down the drive.

'Drive safely!' I shouted after her. She always did, anyway.

I rang to see that she was safely home. There was no reply. I stayed up all night trying her number, though Mark wanted to use the phone to call someone and was impatient with my fussing. That night he slept in the spare room. All through the night I woke and phoned Maggie on the extension phone by my bed. There was no reply.

The next day I rang the police and they told me about the accident. She had been driving carefully, as she always did. The brakes had failed on one of those big articulated lorries whose wheels seem so huge when they thresh past you on the road. The lorry had ploughed across the central reserve of the motorway and hit Maggie's car sideways on. She was dead on arrival. That was what they said: dead on arrival.

I remembered that she said I was a survivor and I thought she would be happy to know that I tried to survive. I went to her funeral and saw her mother and her friends and I told them what she had done for me. How she had broken in when I was such a fool as to hurt myself, how she had held me and rocked me when I could not sleep nor stop crying for Penelope. Then I went home and changed out of the dark black coat and went to a camera shop and bought myself a new lens for my beloved Nikon and started to think what sort of portraits I would like to take now: survivor's pictures.

Mark did not come to the funeral. He said he had to see someone in London at the magazine office, and he could not put them off. I rang him there, but he was not there. The secretary said she had not seen him that day.

He did not come home until late. As soon as he walked into the kitchen I knew where he had been. I could recognise it now, as sharp as a smell around him, as obvious as lipstick on a collar, or perfume on a jacket. He looked petted. He looked glossy. His clear hard profile was somehow softened, as if he had been eating icecream all day and it had melted around his mouth. He looked a little rounder, he looked self-indulgent. When he came to kiss me his breath smelled of sweeties like the breath of a child. He had been sucking peppermints to take away the taint of lunchtime alcohol on his breath. They had probably been drinking champagne in bed while I had been standing at the deep edge of Maggie's grave.

He was not hungry, I threw away his share of the chicken casserole. My own tasted like water. He drank wine while I was eating and then, when we sat together in the sitting room, he glanced sideways at me and told me that he was very very busy on the magazine these days. The circulation figures were rising, and they really should add more pages. And that commuting was such a pain, such a trial.

If I did not object, the magazine's proprietor had offered him the use of the little flat above the office during the week. 'Not every night of course,' he said as I looked from the flames in the fireplace to him. Maybe two, or maybe three nights a week.

'I'll always be home at weekends,' he said, as if he were promising a difficult child a treat for the future.

'And what about Helen?' I asked. The courage I thought I would never find again came unbidden to my hand. Came to me as I sat at my fireside and heard the man I had loved to the point of death and back open his mouth and lie, and lie, and lie.

He flushed scarlet, I could even see it in the dusk. 'I never see her now,' he said.

I nodded. 'And if you're away so much, how would we care for another baby?' I asked. 'When we have another child?'

He smiled at me, his confident smile. 'I think we should wait for a while,' he said. 'It's been very recent . . .' I was glad he did not say her name. 'I know you want another baby but . . .' He broke off. 'Many people think it is better to wait.'

I nodded slowly, watching his smooth smiling face in the firelight. Helen thought it was better to wait. She had taken my husband and now she was denying me my second child.

'You'll start your photography again? It's portraits you want to do now, don't you?' he asked me pleasantly. I could hear Helen's calm planning in every word he said. 'That will mean a change in your technique – you don't want to rush something like that. I met someone today who could perhaps organise a little exhibition if you got some nice pictures together. And I'll see how the expanded magazine goes. Let's wait for a while and see how we feel.'

I knew exactly what he meant.

I should know what I felt by now. I had waited, and waited already.

He meant he would have us both. Helen in town and me in the country. He would weigh us, and taste us, and test us. And then, at the very end of it, he would delay. He would be in no hurry to choose. Mark was not passionately committed as I was . . . as I had been. Mark liked having two women in love with him. It made him feel desirable. I looked at him clearly, and for the first time in my life I truly saw him. I thought of Maggie telling me that I liked chocolate box pictures. I had held in my mind a pretty picture of Mark. I was finished with it now.

'I'll do you a deal,' I offered. The anger in my voice was quite hidden.

'What's that?' He was relieved. He thought he had got away with it. He had wanted this ever since he had started his love affair with Helen, and now he had it. He had to struggle to keep his excitement out of his voice.

'Let me take your picture,' I said. 'With my old camera.'

He laughed. It was such a little thing. He would have sold his soul to sleep in Helen's bed in her Docklands flat, and party with her smart friends all week, and then come home to me, complaisant, ignorant, in the country at weekends.

'Now?' he asked.

'Now!' I said gaily.

I fetched the heavy camera and saw the firelight reflected in a hundred little points on the brass fittings. I ducked under the hood and looked at Mark through the glass window. His image was inverted but I could recognise his expression. He looked like a little boy who has broken into a sweet shop at night. He looked ready to eat himself sick.

I slid in the treated glass, and pulled out the metal slide. I took off the lens cap and counted to sixty – there was only one lamp on, and the firelight. Then I capped the lens with that little half-turn and pushed in the slide and took the glass to develop.

'Will you be long?' Mark called. I heard the chink of the brandy bottle on his glass. 'Are you coming to bed?'

I checked, I could not believe it, but it was true. He wanted to celebrate by having us both, both in the same day. He wanted to kiss me, and caress me while his skin still remembered her touch. He wanted to taste me while his tongue was still furred with the alcohol he had drunk in her bed. He wanted to come inside me, while his body was still sticky from her wetness. He was greedy for us both.

'Don't wait up,' I said from my darkroom.

I printed two pictures. One for me and one for George

Cozens. I pegged them on the line, and I looked, in that safe red light, from the picture of Mark to the pictures of the other two: of my baby and my dearest friend. Both dead.

Then I went to the sitting room and closed the door as quietly as Mark used to close it. I dialled George Cozens' number and when he answered I said I was sorry to ring so late, but it was about the camera. His grandfather had taken very few pictures of people – did George know why that was?

He chuckled, a late-night whisky laugh. 'Because they thought it would steal their souls, you know,' he said. 'Primitive peoples, odd superstitions.'

I nodded. 'I thought so,' I said. 'And one more thing . . . What was the name of the tribe of Indians he photographed? When he *did* manage to get them to pose?'

George hesitated. 'Let me see, they were called the . . . the . . . Ekondo tribe. But there's not much about them in the books,' he said. 'They're all dead now. They died soon after my grandfather's visit.'

'Yes,' I said softly, thinking of the three pictures pinned in my darkroom. My baby, my friend, and now, beside them, the picture of my husband. 'I thought they would be.'

The Garden

My husband is a great one for his garden. He never will let me touch a thing. His garden shed is as he wants it — just so — and he has a greenhouse too, with little plant pots made of orange plastic marching in rows down the staged shelves, which he paints with creosote. The smell of the chemical is like illness. It is coloured a bright green, like toilet cleaner. His greenhouse smells like a morgue.

Every winter he takes the motor mower to be serviced and the blades to be sharpened and made ready for the onslaught of the springing grass when the season opens. He prepares for it like a gamekeeper prepares for a pheasant shoot. All his winter season is directed to the moment when he can get out into the garden and cut it back. He checks the scything whip of the strimmer; he oils and sharpens the crocodile bite of the hedger. Then, on the first sunny day, he tells me he will be gardening all day.

'I can't wait!' he says with his sharp little laugh.

He goes out with his blades and his sprays to work in the garden until teatime. When he comes in for his tea his hands are stained green with sap, like a butcher's palms are reddened with blood. The soft new grass on the lawn is crushed down, the damp earth churned up, the hedge at the front of the house is split and torn, and the soft little corners of the garden where unexceptional plants had taken root and started to grow are laid bare: strimmed and whipped down to the root.

When he sees the devastation he has caused, even he can see that the garden looks a little bare. Then he seeks to fill the vacuum he has made.

'What about one of these swinging chairs?' he asks, showing me a catalogue full of bright plastic.

He thinks to buy me with toys.

'For the patio?' he says. 'This one's nice, and I could get these ornamental urns to match.'

He likes his garden furniture, does my husband. He likes things in the garden that do not loll or sprawl or fruit. He likes plastic statues coloured to look like stone, his flower pots as red as the original terracotta. He likes moulded concrete pots painted to the colour of sandstone. He likes wooden barrels that were never made to hold beer. He does not mind that nothing is what it pretends to be. He does not mind that nothing is real.

Last summer he bought a dinner table and six chairs for the patio. They looked as if they were made of wrought iron, forged and hammered by a man working with iron and fire, cooled in a hissing trough of water. But they were not metal, they were no element at all. At the first wind they were bowled over and blown across the lawn, breaking buds where they rolled, tossed about like a child's discarded toys. They were plastic, they were all but nothing. Now, before he comes in from his garden, he stacks them one upon another like Tupperware boxes on a shelf, and he puts a stone on top to weigh them down.

I remember when he had no garden, when he was nothing more than a lad with an allotment. He took my eye when I stepped off the bus to go home. I was a young woman then, I worked in a shop that sold cards and pens and writing pads. A nice shop, as my mother pointed out to me, with nothing dirty to handle and nothing heavy to lift. Every evening when the bus dropped me at the stop and I started to walk home he would cycle past me, going from his allotment to his own home, where his mother was cooking his tea. Some days he wobbled unevenly with a bouquet of leeks clasped to his shirt. Some days he had a wickerwork basket brimming with new potatoes with the soil still clinging to their skins. In midsummer he embraced a marrow, in autumn he had his arm around the golden globe of a pumpkin. I noticed him because he seemed like a boy from the land itself, as if the allotment had grown him, brown-haired and brown-eyed and muddy-fingered, just as it grew these lush vegetables. And I thought, day-dreamy shop girl that I was, that his kisses might be sweet and strong like vegetables grown in good earth. That to love him might be to put down roots of my own.

It was me that first called out to him. He used to wobble

slowly past me, as if he was thinking what he might say, how he might start a conversation. But it was me, a bit of a brazen girl perhaps, who said pertly enough: 'When are you going to grow some flowers then?'

He stopped at once. 'I don't grow flowers,' he said humbly. 'I don't see the point. You can't eat flowers. Would you like some carrots?'

I laughed at that, but he did not mind. He smiled at my laughter and still he held out for me the earth-stained brilliant carrots with their thick green heads and their long slim orange roots. 'I don't cook,' I said, inspecting them.

'You can eat them raw.'

He took one and rubbed it carefully on the sleeve of his jacket. He held it to my mouth. I nibbled it, like a tempted rabbit, nibbled it gently and tasted the flavour, as sweet as fruit, and the delicious cold chunky texture. 'It's nice,' I said, surprised.

'I'll bring you some peas tomorrow,' he promised me, and then he was back on his bike and gone into the early summer twilight, leaving me with a carrot in my hand, which I ate on the way as I walked slowly home.

He courted me with vegetables, he seduced me as if he came from the earth itself and its fruitfulness was a promise of what our life would be together. By the time he took me home to meet his mother – potato and leek pie – I was already his. I thought that I had found a man who would give me a sense of the earth hidden beneath the pavement, of the richness of a life which had been lost to me, a city-dweller. I thought that we would live off the land, I thought that life would blossom and fruit for us easily, like a paradise, a new Eden. I thought we would eat vegetables and drink water, and riot among grapes and soft fruits.

I was greatly, greatly disappointed. He worked during the day in a shop, just as I did. He worked in a big store, in the accounts department. His real life, the main part of his day, was ceaselessly calculating figures. His excitement was tracing an error in stock or a faulty bill. The allotment was only a hobby, inherited from his father. He had a great love of gardening, but it was not the careless fruitful love that I had hoped for. He liked to struggle with the earth and make it yield only what he ordered. He liked to fight with Nature and subdue it. He liked nothing except what was tamed and trained and trammelled. And in a little while I felt that he wanted me tamed and trained and trammelled too.

I grew thinner. Marriage did not suit me, as it turned out. I who had wanted to luxuriate in fruit and vegetables found that I lost my appetite when offered shop-bought bread and thin cuts of meat. I had hoped to be blessed, rich and fertile. I found that our life was thin and cool, arid. It was no surprise to me that we did not conceive a child. We planned for a child. We bought our house because it had a garden and stood on a new estate where other people with children would come to live. I gave up my job since it was too far for me to travel, and he liked me home in time to prepare his tea. And then we waited for the child.

He waited; not I. I knew that a man who saw himself in a continual battle against Nature would never find me fertile. I knew that a man who liked to cut and weed and hoe would never plant a seed in me. I did nothing to prevent it. I simply knew that it could not happen. And when it did not happen, I felt neither disappointment nor surprise. I felt myself slip into a sort of limbo while I waited to see what would happen next. But it was years ago that I started waiting to see what would happen next. And the answer was that nothing happened next. Nothing much changed at all – except the garden.

When he first bought this house it stood in a sea of churned earth where a wood had once grown. Corrugated tracks ran around it and the rubble from the builders cluttered the two corners that faced out from the housing estate to the woods. My husband paced out the boundaries and marked where his mud joined next door's mud. He stuck little white stakes into the earth and measured up, he bought fence posts and fencing, so our churned earth would be separated from the other churned earth, and from the untouched woodlands behind the house. Nothing mattered more to him than he should mark out our land, defend it from the incursions of next door – whoever they might prove to be – and cleanse it of the anarchic influence of the woods.

But that first spring, while he measured and paced and staked, the garden flowered without him, it flowered despite him, and day after day I watched the woodland flowers creeping into the sun like fifth columnists from the old wood.

Snowdrops came first, with sharp determined spoonheads forcing their way through the mud. Then the knives of daffodil leaves sprouted blind thick leaves that swelled and swelled in the sunlight, pregnant with hidden blooms.

'Someone's gardened here before!' my husband said indignantly. 'They promised me that this was nothing but fields before they built the estate, but look here – there are bulbs all over!'

He went to telephone, to discover the price of a Rotavator to tear the earth away from the alien flowers, but they were too quick and cunning for him. While he argued with the shopmen and checked the catalogues, the rosettes of primroses threw out pale hairy stalks and Caerphilly cheese-coloured flowers, violets cropped in the shade of his new fence, and a thick carpet of vetch as blue as a midsummer night sky spread around the marking posts which were defining the site of his ornamental lily pond.

Nettles sprouted in thick green clumps, juicy with stings, and his garden gloves could not shield his burrowing hands from their rich malice. He came to tea with a face red and moist with anger. 'Don't you worry,' he said. 'I'll see to them. We'll see how they like a can of X.30.'

He made the poison at my kitchen sink, in my pastry bowl. I watched him as he handled the powder, dribbling in water in a measured dose. When I looked out of the window a breeze stirred the nettles and the forget-me-nots that had filtered among them, and they trembled and shrank back.

Next morning they were all brown and limp, rotting where they lay, like some mediaeval battlefield struck with plague. He had sprayed wildly with his pump-gun and the acid had eaten into the faces of the pansies. The primrose leaves were sere and yellow and the flowers brown as paper. He sprayed again the next night, and the night after, until the garden was sick to its secret heart and everything there was dead. Then, at last, was my husband finally happy and he dug a large hole for his lily pond and ordered the men with concrete to come and level the diseased soil in front of the patio doors and pour the concrete like molten lava to bury everything, so that nothing, not even the tiniest hidden root of a tenacious primrose, could survive.

And I knew then, as they wiped out the life for yards around the house, that I had been mistaken in him. 'What would happen next' was nothing more than this realisation. He was not a lad enriched with the earth, warm from the vegetable bed. He had looked like that to me in the seductive dusk of a summer evening; but I had been wrong. He had never been a young man who would bring me the richness of the earth, I would not be able to grow old with him and mellow like the bloom on an autumn grape. I had not lived the life I had hoped for, I would not have a future that would bring me joy. My husband had looked like a lad as sweet as a plum but he had become a middle-aged man who suspected richness, who was afraid of life. He liked killing the flowers; he liked crushing the life out of the earth. He watched them pouring the concrete into the marked squares with vindictive joy.

'Now we're getting somewhere!' he said. He was delighted.

He has never encouraged me to garden. In our marriage the world is divided into those things which are my work, and those things which belong to him. It is more orderly thus. The money he earns is his, of course. He gives me cash every Monday for the shopping and once a fortnight he takes the household bills to the kitchen table and writes out cheques to cover them. It is my job to put the cheques in the envelopes and make sure that they are posted.

The car is his, owned and driven and maintained by him. When I drive it he tells me what I am doing wrong and where it should be parked. He tells me which lane I should be in, and whether or not it is safe to reverse. When it makes a rattley noise he names parts of the engine which might be causing that noise. He takes it to the garage and they pretend to listen to him, and nod in agreement. Then they do whatever they want and send him an enormous bill, which he pays without regret. He knows about cars and how to drive because he is a man, just as I do not know because I am a woman.

The television is his; he watches every night from teatime till bedtime, the remote control is on the arm of his chair, he changes the programme without discussion, and I know, without ever being told, that there are some programmes that he must see, that must not be interrupted even by a remark. I sit in silence and my face is turned towards the screen but I do not always see the pictures.

The whole lounge is his, for I never sit there alone. Actually, I never sit down for very long during the day; even my dinner is a sandwich I eat while I am working.

But my husband is a great one for his chair. He dominates the room from his place by the fire and the television, with the coffee table conveniently close and the magazine rack to hand. It is his own chair, a special chair where no-one else sits, and as well as this chair, he has his own place at the kitchen table, at the head of the table furthest away from the sink and the oven. He has his own side of the bed, beside the bedside table and his reading light. The bathroom is his because he controls how it should look. It is tiled and plain, he cannot abide clutter in the bathroom. We have small bath towels, he says large thick towels are a pointless extravagance, copied from American films. I am allowed one brand of bath salts, which must be put into a special jar that sits on the side of the bath, one jar only. I cannot have oils and salts and foam. I have to choose one product and stick with it. He does not want disorder in the bathroom.

It is his garden, of course, and his garage.

In this division of goods I own nothing but somehow I am responsible for it all. I keep his special chair clean, Hoovering up crumbs from the interstices of the cushions.

The Garden

◈

I polish his television screen carefully to make sure there are no distracting smears. I clean his bathroom, taking care with the underside of the toilet seat which he will see when he lifts and leaves it up; changing the empty rolls for fresh toilet paper, changing the towelling top and the towelling mat around the base twice a week, for men are careless in these trivial matters and it is often spattered with his urine. I clean the bedside table where he sometimes leaves his torn toenails. I buy him a new toothbrush when his old one is squashed. I clean the bath every day and the sink where he leaves a light line of shaving foam and stubble. And it is my task to throw away his old razor blades, which he leaves greasy and still spitefully sharp on the windowsill.

The cooker is mine, I suppose. The sink, the larder, the fridge, the Hoover, the mop, the kitchen cupboards, the washing machine, the tumble dryer. The electricity to run these goods is his – I must be frugal with his supply. Washing must dry on the rotary washing line that grows like a bleak espaliered tree from the concrete slab outside the back door.

The washing machine must work through the night on cheap rate electricity. The central heating system is his, it switches itself off as he departs in the morning, and comes on only as he arrives home at night. I sometimes think that the house is applauding his return. The boiler gives a little 'huff' and roars into life half an hour before I hear his key in the lock. The house readies itself for the return of the owner.

'It's a waste to heat the whole house all day when you only use the kitchen,' he tells me. As the house cools around me all day I cling to the little convector heater in the kitchen and make little sorties into the cold bedrooms to Hoover and wipe down and dust.

The telephone too is his; I rob him every time I make a call. I telephone only when he is out of the house, and I put down the receiver when I hear his car in the drive. To see me start at the sound of the boiler coming on and quickly finish my call would make anyone would think that I am keeping a secret; but I am not. The only secret is that sometimes I need to hear my own voice. Sometimes I long to hear myself talk and laugh and gossip as if I were happy. As if it were my telephone and I had friends to call.

He knows that I use it when he is out of the house. He has put a timer beside it. I am supposed to turn the dial to 3 every time I make a local call. I am not supposed to make any national calls until after midday, or preferably after six. 'If you must phone your sister, do it at the weekend,' my husband says when he opens the telephone bill. Then he always says as a joke the slogan they use on children's programmes when they invite children to call in: 'Always get permission from whoever pays the bill.'

When I first saw the house, with the low sweeping branches of the untouched wood overhanging the rich churned earth, I thought we had bought a house in the forest, with trees within touching distance of my door. But he hired a chain saw and amputated them one Saturday morning, working without a break from quarter to nine till after one, in a frenzy of noise, in a cloud of dim blue exhaust fumes, while one branch after another tore, split, fell.

He piled the wood into a pyre on the poisoned earth, soaked it with petrol from the chainsaw – 'No reason to give them back the unused fuel!' he said cleverly – and burned it all, burned it all up, until there was nothing but a pile of pale woodash, soft as talcum powder, and nothing left of the trees but white scarred limbs where the branches had once bent low and whispered with their leaves to the grasses and the little hidden flowers.

I closed the door against the haunting scent of wood-smoke. It stung my eyes and made them as red as if I had been crying for the trees which I thought would blow gently around my new house.

My husband is a great one for his garden. He never will let me touch a thing, and when the trees were wounded, the ground poisoned, when the wild flowers drooped their scarred heads and wilted, and the thick plastic tub of the lily pond was lowered into place, then I felt I did not want to touch his garden. I did not want to sit in his garden, I felt as if the dead earth beneath the concrete mock-cobble finish had died of some disgusting injury, like gangrene from a rotting limb. And as it slowly died, something of my pallid spirit died too.

He tried to tempt me with his shoddy chairs. With his blow-away dining table, with his twin-wheeled barbecue set. 'Come and see the lily pond, it looks a picture!'

I went to see. It was easier than saying 'no'. There were two ominous watery growths in small plastic crates. Their roots trailed like sly watersnakes across the azure floor of the pond. 'Put a couple of koi carp in there,' my husband says proudly. 'Think how they'll look!'

I know how they will look. They will gaze up at me; their goggling bemused eyes wide and despairing. They will swim round and round their plastic prison, finning through the grasping roots of the lily plants. I do not think I can bear it, to share the poisoned garden with two prisoners. But I say nothing. The garden is his.

Now he buys plants. Rack upon rack of bedding plants he buys from the garden centre and brings them home like kidnapped children, alien force-bred seedlings, each in a polystyrene pot like strange lonely growths from a science lab. He taps them out into his hand, and crushes them into the flowerbed, one and then another, and another. When he comes in for his tea I look out of the patio window and see another little row of helpless soldiers, marching along the strict line of grass. Limp and lost.

I have taken to straying.

A gap opened up in his fence. It is behind his potting shed and he has not yet seen it. Some dog in the night has wriggled between two newly creosoted six-by-five panels of fencing, and left a gap. I am thin, as thin as a child now, and I can bend the fence back and slide through. In the afternoons, when I should be ironing his shirts that have washed all night and danced on the scaffold of the dryer all morning, I bend back the fence, and slip through and out to the woodland.

It is only a small wood. Our housing estate encroaches on the west side, to the south are fenced fields and then the town. To the east and north there are roads and houses. But it is a very old wood. The trees are thick-trunked, mossy, tall. There is a yew tree with branches as lush as a jungle, blackly green. There are oak trees with mangled craggy bark; there are beech trees, half a dozen within whispering distance of each other. The silver birches shiver their heart-shaped leaves, in every corner. There are many birds, they whisper and sing in secret places. The forest floor is soft with dried leaves, mossy by the drainage ditch that is full of stagnant water and wriggling life. And in the heart of this little wood, where no-one walks but me, where there are no paths but the faint print of my house slippers on rustling leaves, in the heart of this little wood there is a fallen tree where I lie on my back, stretch out and look up through the branches to the sky.

'Where were you this afternoon?' he asks at teatime. 'I telephoned you, I needed the Bullens' address.'

'In the garden,' I say quickly, without thinking.

'You didn't touch anything, did you?' he asks, immediately anxious. 'I have a plan for all the plants. You have to keep on top of a garden, you know.'

'I didn't touch anything,' I say.

◆

I look past him to the garden through the patio window. He has planted gladioli and iris in strict painful rows and their little green heads are pushing through the earth, viewing the close-mowed grass, and the marching ranks of the limp-leafed bedding plants.

'What it is to be a lady of leisure!' he says like a joke. But it is not a joke. He will be watching now, for some chore left undone. He spends the evening looking around the room, and he is triumphant when at bedtime he thinks he has caught me out.

'I need black socks for tomorrow,' he beams. 'I always wear black socks on Fridays, to go with my black suit. Branch meeting on Fridays, I always wear my black suit.'

'They're airing,' I say. 'They'll be ready tomorrow morning.'

He gives a short laugh. 'All that lazing around in the afternoon,' he says. 'And now we see who pays the price!'

I smile as if I believe he is joking. His face is sharp, like a keen little rodent. 'Did you bring the cushions in?' he asks suddenly. 'After you had finished sitting in my garden? Did you bring the cushions in and put them in the right place in the cupboard under the stairs?'

'Yes,' I say. In my mind I can see the flutter of the green leaves of the beech trees as they interlaced the sky above my upturned face. The sunlight flickered through them into my eyes; it was as green as leaves, that light. But when I closed my eyes against its brightness there were circling moons of blood red on my eyelids.

He goes to the bathroom with a magazine. I know by this that he is moving his bowels and he will be there for a long time.

When he flushes the handle and comes out the seat will be intimately warm and the air will smell stale and old. I sit and wait on the edge of the bed until he has finished in the bathroom. Even the time that I may sleep is dictated by him.

I wake in the night with a start. The curtains have parted and the moon is shining full upon my face, as imperative as a tug on the sleeve. My husband is on his back, his mouth is open, his tongue slack. He breathes out loudly, and then snorts in through his nose. I turn away from him and look at the moon.

I have never seen it so close, it seems impossible that it should be so close, it is drawing closer and closer, ready to settle on the wood itself, it will drown us in its blue and white radiance. I can see the shapes and shadows of it. I can see every little contour. They have all been mapped and named, foolish names, pompous names, names chosen by men trained as scientists but trying to be lyrical, men straining for effect. Tonight I can see it as if it were taking revenge for being landed on. Tonight it is going to land on me.

I slide out of bed. I am so thin that I barely shift the covers. I put my towelling dressing gown around me and tie the belt tight. I go downstairs barefoot. The patio doors are well oiled, they do not squeak when I push them backwards. Then I step out into his garden in the moonlight.

In the coolness of the white light I can see the damage he has done. The little plants cast helpless shadows, like one blot after another in a rigorous line. The iris and the gladioli stand like sentries behind the bowed heads of the pansies, of the daisies, of the staked and spiked clumps of wallflowers. The water lilies in their cages in his pond spread their waxy flowers on the trapped water, the little cherry tree in the corner has spread two spindly branches and put out rosy despairing buds like fingers clawing for release. In the moonlight I can hear them all, I can hear them all calling to me.

He has a wheelbarrow, a large wheelbarrow. I am suddenly able and quick, I go to his garden shed and I take out his shining spade. In the moonlight it is silver, sharpened silver, like a sword. I take the little tree first, digging down to gather all its roots. As I thought, it has kept the shape of its pot, it has not dared to spread its roots into the earth he poisoned, it was never planted; just laid to rest in his dead garden. It lifts easily from the pot-shaped grave and I put it in the wheelbarrow.

I am stronger than I have dreamed. I dig for the iris, for the gladioli. They come up easily, gladly, as if they were escaping from the sourness of his earth. They leave gaping holes like empty catacombs. I go to the fence. I cannot squeeze the barrow through the gap. I have to take a panel of the fence down. I struggle with it – it is heavy and well set. I feel as if I am breaking a prison wall. When it lurches to one side and falls I can hear them cheer in their soft voices.

I trundle the barrow into the wood, across the rustling leaves, over the wet moss. My feet are smeared with mud and my dressing-gown hem is embroidered with soil and leaf mold. For the first time in years I can feel myself growing wet between my legs and when I laugh it is a breathless sound of an aroused girl.

I have brought the spade and I dig a deep hole for the cherry tree. When I set it down I can see its roots stretch out, snake towards the good untouched earth. Around it I plant the iris and gladioli, I watch their heads rise under the shower of moonlight, grow straighter, sweeten. I weave between the trees with his wheelbarrow. I do not want a path to mark these woods. I must be devious, cunning.

I use a trowel to steal his bedding plants. They come to my hand like trusting small birds. I pile them, limp and wan as they are, into the belly of the wheelbarrow until it is filled with their bodies. Then I take them to the heart of the wood and clear pockets in the leaves for them. I set them deep in the clean earth, jostling each other at random. Broken out from their ranks they look like living things at last. I can see their leaves spread, taking their own space. There is a strange wild sound in the moonlit wood and I realise it is my voice singing.

Lastly I take the caged water lilies and tear the plastic pots away from their sweet white roots. They wrap around my hands like snakes as I plunge them into the drainage ditch. I see them dip and sway on the stagnant water. I see them spread their net of roots. Little water boatmen swim under their leaves, the flowers open under the moonlight and I can smell a faint potent sexual scent.

Last of all I take the koi carp in a bucket and tip them into the ditch. They flicker out of sight into the green depths of the water. They do not look at me. They do not mirror my old anxious goggling face. They are free.

Very quietly, I take the wheelbarrow home, wipe the handles, wipe the spade and the trowel. It is a forensic exercise; I am copying his television programmes. No one will find a trace of the crime on me.

The garden is a desert pitted with holes where the plants were once imprisoned. It looks like a sacked town, like a broken jail. The plastic chairs stand guard over gaping holes. The concrete cobbles edge empty beds. The blind statues see nothing in the moonlight.

I put the fence back in its place. I rake and then sweep away the track made by the wheels of the barrow. Nothing can tell him where the plants have gone. He will believe it is the envy of neighbours, the malice of vandals, the misplaced humour of spiteful children. The plants are hidden. They are safe from him. They are a secret garden, as far from him as Eden.

I wash my hands, my face, I brush my hair and leaves fall from my head as if I were a tree-woman. I pick them off the bathroom floor and hide them in the wastepaper bin. My spattered dressing gown goes in the washbasket, I slide into bed beside his stiff sleeping body and I turn my face to the setting moon and close my eyes. I am exhausted by joy. I fall asleep at once.

Tomorrow I shall sit in my secret garden.
   Tomorrow and everyday.

The Last Swan

◆

I was eight when I started at the Siddleset Ducklings. You could join at six, so when I arrived there was already an established clique of arrogant little girls who had their favourite locker and their favourite peg in the changing room, and whose mothers had their favourite seat at the side of the corporation swimming pool. On Monday night the pool was closed to ordinary people, only the swimming clubs were allowed in. It was quite something to be in the swimming clubs in Siddleset, even if you were only the newest Siddleset Duckling.

The teacher of the Siddleset Synchronised Swimming Club called herself Madame Louisa, and all us Ducklings called her Madame. She was French and she had taught ballet before she fell in love with water – she said that, not me. She always talked like that. 'I fall in love with water,' she would say, spreading her arms wide as if the Siddleset Corporation Baths were some mystical elemental force. 'And so now I share my passion for ballet and my passion for water and I teach my girls to dance in the water.'

If the teams hadn't been so successful they wouldn't have stood for this in Siddleset, which is a no-nonsense sort of market town south of Darlington. But they were successful: county champions three times running, national runners-up twice, and last year Moira Field won Most Promising Newcomer at the national competition, and Madame said she was certain to win the National Synchronised Solo Swim in the summer.

We all warmed up together on the side of the pool and did our stretching exercises and then us Ducklings swam first, while the others did stamina exercises. Then we got dry and changed and came out to our row of chairs by the poolside. We were expected to wait till the Cygnets had finished and then watch the Swans do their routine. 'You learn by observation,' Madame said. 'So observe. Swim in your minds. Swim in your minds.'

I never minded waiting, because if I waited I would see Moira Field. I loved Moira Field. She was the most beautiful girl in Siddleset. Out of the water she didn't look much, but when she had her cap on, and her nose clip on, and she went underwater, you could see then that she was the most beautiful girl on the team and probably the most beautiful girl in the world. She could hold her breath for ages, and sometimes, when she was underwater and her white pointed feet were criss-crossing above the surface of the pool, you would think she would drown before coming up.

Madame liked Moira Field too. Everyone liked her.

Madame was sure she would win the National Solo Synchronised Swim and then everyone would know about the Siddleset Swans, and we would all have our picture in the paper.

Us Ducklings had our competition routine as well. We swam to 'Down in the Meadow in the little Fishy Pool . . .' It was really babyish, we hated it. We had to stand on the edge and flap our elbows like ducks before we jumped in the water and did our swim. It was stupid and none of us liked it. 'Smile!' Madame would say. 'Look happy! It is a playful little dance for the Ducklings!' We did as she said but we thought it was stupid. We all wanted to be one of the Cygnets team who had 'Fame! I'm going to live forever . . .' which was brilliant, and they did a little disco dance before they dived in. They were allowed to dive, while we were only allowed to jump. Things like that matter when you're a synchronised swimmer.

None of us wanted anything as much as we wanted to be in the Cygnets. We never even thought about the Swans. They were as far above us as stars above the roof of the Corporation Baths. They had three different costumes, all with millions of sequins sewn on by hand. They didn't wear caps at competitions but gelled up their hair with special waterproof hair gel. They wore special waterproof makeup which they painted on with little sponges, all over their faces and their necks and even their shoulders. They had three events: one for the full team, one for half the team, and one for a pair. Then Moira did her solo.

There were other solo dancers in the team; but none like Moira. No-one else could stay underwater as long. No-one else's arabesques were as straight or as still. When she was right way up she smiled with such serenity that there was no way you could tell that her legs were barrelling away underwater. When she did her leap out of the water with her hands above her head it looked as if someone had lifted her and flung her upwards, she went so high. When she swam out at the end she might be out of puff but you could never tell. She was still smiling.

'To the changing room, hold that smile to the changing room . . .' Madame would call, and Moira would smile and smile her blank glassy beautiful smile until she got to the changing room and turned into an ordinary, slightly flat-footed sixth former again. She was a bit plump when she wasn't in the water, in her outdoor clothes she looked like any other lacklustre schoolgirl. But with her makeup covering her slightly speckled skin, and her hair gelled into a waterproof helmet, and her nose pinched tight by her nose clip, she was a beautiful girl. 'An artiste,' Madame said. 'I will make you an artiste.'

Her solo was to 'Endless Love'; it was just beautiful. It was very slow – and that's one of the hardest things to do. She had to hold her positions for ages. But the music was so thick and loud it was like soup, like creamy soup. When you listened and you saw Moira go into her first arabesque it was as if the music went in through your ears, and the point of her extended toe went in through your eyes, and they joined together in your brain, and you could see and hear and think of nothing else.

Moira always did her solo last of all, after warm-up and stamina work, and the team dances. All us Ducklings would ask our mums if we could stay until Moira had finished. I liked to stay until she came out of the water (smiling, smiling all the way to the changing room) so I could hand her towel to her, and see her face, still pinched sharp by her nose clip, turn towards me for one brief dismissive moment. 'Thank you,' she would say, and then I would go home with my mum, and my dad would say, 'Good swim?' and I would say, 'Wonderful.' But I knew he would never understand, and I would never explain.

We were working towards the Nationals in July, and Madame was more and more demanding at every swimming session from May onwards. She got really cross with the Cygnets for mucking about in the changing rooms. She shouted at them and even said things in French. One of the mums was upset, but the others knew it was just Madame's way before a big event. She had all the worry of it. And with Moira going for the National Solo title this year, well, everyone knew how serious it was. The Swans team were really nasty to the Cygnets when they came in to change and found water all over the floor. They called them stupid kids and complete pains. Us Ducklings just kept out of the way.

Then in June, at the first training session of the month, there was a dreadful notice pinned on the pool door, and

the door was shut. Madame was ill, and there was no training, even though it was Monday, and the competition only
a month away. She had fallen and broken her hip and gone
to hospital. All the mums stood around outside the door,
and the Swans and the Cygnets and us Ducklings peered
through the double glass doors trying to see the pool. It
was awful being shut out, it was awful having to go home
without having swum, and awful to see Moira only in her
boring white aertex shirt and navy blue skirt looking plain
and dull, turning around and biking home, just like
anybody.

But during the week the club found a new trainer. A
man trainer. 'That'll shake 'em up,' Dad said. I didn't know
that men knew anything about synchronised swimming. I
thought it was all women, except for the judges. There
weren't any boy swimmers, and the dads only came to
competition nights. I didn't know that men knew how to
do it.

He was nice. He said, 'Call me Steve,' which seemed
very odd. He knew different warm-up exercises and they
were good fun, and he didn't do stamina exercises at all,
he threw weights down to the bottom of the pool and made
us fetch them, and threw floating hoops in and we had to
swim through them. It was really good fun, like playing.
I wondered what Madame would say about people splashing
and laughing in training. Some of the youngest Ducklings
got really silly and over-excited, and had to be ducked to
make them shut up.

He watched the routines and he liked the Ducklings, he even laughed at the little duck dance, which I didn't like because synchronised swimming ought to be serious. But when he came to the Swans he shook his head.

'This is something like ten years out of date,' he said.

Then he saw Moira's solo and I could tell that he didn't like it either. That was when I knew that I didn't like him. He didn't say anything but he called us altogether at the poolside. Us Ducklings were dressed and ready to go home. The Cygnets and the Swans had their towels around them. I gave Moira her towel and for once she didn't say thank you. She just took it. She was looking at him, at Steve.

'You're a great team,' he said. 'I wouldn't have come to train you if I hadn't known that. You're a great team. Stamina good, lines excellent, formation excellent. What I want us to work on between now and the competition is making you a bit more up to date.'

He said that synchronised swimming was making a bid, a big bid, to be taken seriously as a sport. That it was an Olympic sporting event and it must stay in the Olympics. That people thought it was a load of silly girls with sequins and that it was our job to show them that it was a major strand of athletics and swimming. When he said that, about sequins, I looked at Moira. She had three beautiful costumes and she was making a new one for the Nationals in July. I knew that it would be covered with sequins, and Madame had shown her how to put them on her hairband too, so she had sequins in her hair.

One of the girls had some waterproof glue so that you could stick sequins on your eyebrows. I couldn't imagine that Moira could win without her sequins, I even thought she might sink without them.

'So I've got some new music, and a new design,' Steve said. 'Moira and the Swans, stay behind and I'll play it to you. Cygnets and Ducklings, see you next week. You've done very well. I'm very pleased with you.'

That night, Dad said, 'Good swim?' and I said, 'All right.' But I did not feel all right. I felt that things were going wrong.

Next Monday we all stayed behind to watch Moira's new solo. The music was 'Pumping Iron' and she started it in the water, so you didn't really get to see the costume, or her dive in. It just looked like the stamina exercises to me, over and over again. Lots of underwater work, and lots of high jumps. It was really hard, we could tell that. When she came out she was panting, I'd never seen her like that before. She couldn't catch her breath to smile at all, never mind smile smile smile all the way to the changing rooms.

'That's great,' Steve said. 'You've worked really hard. No-one expects you to look as if you've just been for a stroll. Keep those feet moving, keep breathing, excellent.'

I held out her towel for her, and I saw her face. Her face was scarlet with the effort of the new routine. She did not look serene and beautiful, she looked exhausted. She pulled off the nose clip and her nose was an angry red, her eyes were watery from the chlorine.

'It's not "Come Dancing" any more,' he said. 'It's not pretty-pretty waving your arms around. It's not cutaway swimsuits and showing your legs to the judges like underwater Tiller girls. It's a sport. It's about discipline, and stamina, and ability. Just like the long jump or the parallel bars, or a freestyle race. You can do it. You can all do it. And we'll win at the National Championships, I guarantee it.'

He took the tape out of the machine and passed it to Moira. 'Train at home to it,' he said. 'Get that beat and get moving to it.'

She wiped her hand on the towel and took it from him, reluctantly, as if she did not really want it. 'It's loud and hard and happening,' he said. 'The Mantovani sound is yesterday's swimming, Moira. I promise you.'

'Yes,' she said. 'Thank you.'

The next three weeks we worked harder than we had ever worked for Madame. He choreographed the Swans dance again, and they were swimming to a rap number now. He wanted us all in regulation black Speedo swimsuits. 'This is sports,' he said. 'Not a fashion parade.' Some of the Ducklings were quite tearful in the changing room.

We had been promised a white costume with silver sequins, and little white net wings on the shoulder straps. The Swans were sulky and changed in silence. Some of them liked the new dance but none of them liked the costume. They had been going to wear their blue – very high-cut at the leg and with a swathe of green and blue sequins from hip to shoulder. 'Too 1950s,' Steve said, and it made it worse that no-one knew what he meant.

The Nationals were held at Filton Pool, Bristol. The teams went all together on the coach and the mums and dads came on later, by car. I was really nervous but when I heard the 'Three Little Fishes' song I sort of floated away and did the whole dance and swim in a dream. Everyone clapped a lot, and then we got fifth place which was brilliant because the Ducklings had never been placed before. The Cygnets got tenth place, which everyone said was unfair, and happened only because one of the judges preferred the Plymouth team, and she had been coaching there in the spring. So it wasn't fair at all.

Then it was the Swans with their team event, and they took fourth place and we all screamed 'Yessss!' and clapped and clapped. The pair swim went all wrong, and weren't placed, and then it was the solo.

I saw at once that Steve was right. The solo pieces were all very athletic and energetic. They splashed like mad – and we had always been taught never to splash. They spent ages underwater and they did a lot of leaps. It was not like Madame's style at all. It was not like Moira.

I didn't think she could swim like that, not even with the 'Pumping Iron' music and the new choreography. Not well enough to be placed anyway.

When they called her I was looking at the spectator gallery, and I didn't see her come out of the changing room. By the time I saw her she was at the poolside, and I gasped.

She wasn't wearing what she had been given and she didn't look how she was supposed to look at all.

She should have been in a neat black costume with a black rubber cap, her face scrubbed bare of makeup, and her fingernails pale. But she was not. She looked like a mermaid escaped from a dream aquarium. Her costume was a shimmering hail of sequins, in deep iridescent blue. It was cut high up to her hips and low at the front to show a fleshy substantial cleavage painted a smooth uniform pink. Her hair was gelled into a perfectly solid mass of a French pleat surrounded by curls like the twirls on a cast-iron gate. Each hairgrip skewering each lock into place was studded with a sparkly flower made of sequins and glitter. She had got hold of the waterproof glue and her eyebrows were made from overlapping green and blue sequins, her eyeliner was a thick line of pure silver. Her thick waterproof makeup made her face, her neck, her shoulders, even her arms, a solid pleasing pink. Her lips – first outlined firmly in pencil, painted with lipstick, and shiny from the final coat of lip-gloss – were an uncompromising fuschia. Her eyes either side of the sharp pinched nose were deep wells of matte blue eye shadow from the socket to the lid. Her eyelashes were monstrous extravagances, superbly long, superbly thick, superbly black.

Steve lunged for her but he was too late. Her music, her *real* music, boomed out over the loudspeakers: 'Endless Love'. She posed by the ringside, like a statue of a perfect goddess, and then dived her beautiful straight-legged deep dive, like a blue gannet, straight into the water.

She did her dance, Madame's dance, flawlessly. She extended her hands, with deep shiny blue nails, high into the air. She upended and pointed her scissoring red-painted toes to the sky. She re-emerged smiling her serene smile, while her legs churned under the water, keeping her steady, keeping her in place. She soared up into her leap, clasped her hands above her head and sank like an arrow under the water, emerged, turned, somersaulted, and the painted smile never even wavered.

The dance finished. Holding her smile, she swam slowly to the steps. There was a smatter of tentative applause and then as she rose from the water she heard the long condemning silence, echoey as a cathedral in the tall silent swimming pool. The judges bent their heads and whispered among themselves, Steve turned his back to her, he would not look at her. She knew, she must have known, that she was disgraced, completely and utterly; and she would never swim for the Siddleset Swans ever again.

But I knew, when I saw her rise from the greeny water of the pool, not a hair out of place, not a sequin disturbed, that I had seen a model of womanhood at the moment of extinction. Like an exquisite dinosaur she stood, her smile as serene as if she were being offered the homage that was unquestionably her due, ignoring the furious rejection of Steve, ignoring the black looks of the judges, ignoring the uneasy ominous silence of the crowd, the shrinking of her friends. Her eyelids, heavily freighted by the waterlogged weight of the massive false eyelashes, loaded with eye-shadow, eyeliner and waterproof mascara on the top, gazed blindly out over the water, as if she were dreaming of a world where she would be accepted – even applauded – for such a triumph of Art over Nature. Where people understood that womanhood, perfect womanhood, must be arduously constructed.

She turned and looked for her towel, still smiling; her huge painted eyes filled with chlorine and tears. Whatever the result, whatever insulting score they levelled at her, she would smile, smile all the way to the changing room, and I knew that whatever I became in the future, when I was no longer a Siddleset Cygnet, nor even a Siddleset Swan, that I had seen tonight an image of womanhood which I would revere in my heart. I would cherish this picture of her – forever.

I stepped forward and gave her the towel, and I felt myself bob in the little curtsey which Madame had taught us, the curtsey for use when presenting a bouquet of flowers to minor royalty.

'Thank you,' Moira said graciously, without looking at me. She was still smiling.

The Bimbo

◆

The men in the office all went bananas when Bambi arrived. It was absurd, but that was her name. She was our new temp: Bambi Summers. I called her into my office and she came in smoothing down her skirt all the way over her knickers – no further. There were yards of thigh on view.

I didn't mind. I'm at a level of success in my life – a partnership in the law firm, a solid relationship with my colleague Philip, an established life of my own. A pretty blonde with huge blue eyes and legs which go on forever doesn't frighten me. Irritates: yes. Frightens: no.

'What's your proper name?' I asked. 'Your real name? I can't call you Bambi. This is a legal firm and you will be working as my clerk. We don't use pet-names.'

'My real name *is* Bambi,' she said. 'My mum loves the film. She wanted to call my brother Thumper but the register wouldn't let her.'

'Regis*trar*,' I said.

'Thumper,' she said.

There was a short pause.

'Don't you have another name, a proper name?'

'No,' she said. She looked rather hurt. 'Won't you please call me Bambi, Miss Cook? Everyone does.'

'All right,' I said. 'But you must tell the clients that your name is Miss Summers.'

She nodded obediently and I felt ungracious.

'And what do I call you?' she asked.

'You call me Miss Cook.'

I had expected that she would be incompetent, and I was ready to send her back to the temp company with an acid request that they supply someone more suitable for an old established legal firm; but she was an ideal typist. She worked at remarkable speed and she never made a single mistake. She kept a dictionary on her desk and if she didn't know a word, she looked it up. There were many words she didn't know, but she learned them fast. It was only her speech which was sloppy and her dress which was outrageous. Her work was immaculate.

If she had been any less thorough I would have sacked her. The last thing I needed was all the senior partners popping their heads around the door of the clerks' office and saying 'Hello Bambi' in artificial high voices as if they were cooing to a baby.

Philip was as bad as any of them. I pretended that I hadn't noticed; but he called in to her office first thing every morning to pick up his post and stayed longer and longer every day. I have perfectly good legs myself but the criminal court is hardly the place for them. I wear long skirts and thick tights at work. Beside my dull blackbird appearance Bambi was a budgie, a little songbird, a pet.

And they petted her; all the men in the office did. They teased her and made funny telephone calls to her pretending to be clients and confessing to murder and bigamy. She was fooled every time – she didn't just pretend to be naive to egg them on. She would come scuttering into my office on her kitten heels and say: 'Miss Cook! Miss Cook! There's a man on the phone who says he's a monogamist! Should I call the police?'

When I told her it was one of the partners teasing her she would collapse into giggles and go and look up monogamist in her dictionary. I would hear her whoop of laughter as she finally got the joke five minutes late.

When the senior partners went out for lunch they would bring back the chocolate mints from their coffee saucers, and she would thank them as if they had given her a box of Belgian chocolates. One of them, I think it may have been Philip, put a plant in her office: a heady sweet-smelling white gardenia.

It grew warmer and then the trees outside the office in the square became lush and green. Bambi's skirts could not go any shorter; but she wore little crop tops which skimmed the brow of her navel and stretched and moved interestingly as she walked. Her flat stomach was light brown, her arms were the colour of well-made toast, downy with fair hair. She was a caramel cream toasting in the sunshine. Every lunchtime she took a can of a fizzy drink and a sandwich and lay in the full sun in the gardens of the square, and Philip, coming back from court, would sit beside her, still wearing his black gown, and pick blades of grass, and talk to her.

I had a case to defend in the Midlands and I was away for the week. When I came back, tired and travel-worn, pale from the long days in court, Philip had written me a letter and Bambi had a large white diamond on her hand.

She put her head around my door with her apologetic little-girl expression. 'I hope you're not mad at me,' she said.

'D'you really think he means to marry you?' I didn't feel jealousy as much as a cold curiosity.

She gave a little gasp. 'Oh! He has to!'

I was stunned that Philip had been such a fool. 'You can get rid of it,' I said baldly. 'It's perfectly easy. You don't even have to stay in hospital overnight these days. Philip would certainly pay.'

She looked at me as if I were speaking another language. 'What d'you mean?' she asked.

Then: 'Oh! You think I am pregnant?'

She looked deeply shocked. 'It's not *that*,' she said earnestly. 'It's not that at all! I meant that he has to marry me because I love him. I love him so much,' she said. '*So much.*'

We looked at each other with mutual incomprehension. She knew a Philip that I had never met, although we had been friends and colleagues for three years and lovers for one. The Philip who dined with me on alternate Saturday nights and then cooked breakfast with me on Sunday mornings could not have inspired that gasp of longing. My Philip was an efficient lawyer, a cool head, a temperate lover, and a reliable friend.

'Don't you know?' she asked in simple wonderment. 'You've known him so long. Don't you feel the same about him? He's so wonderful!'

I shook my head. 'But why marry?' I asked. 'Why don't you just live with him? If you're so much in love.'

She blushed scarlet as if I had said something deeply improper. 'I don't want to just live with him, I want to be his wife,' she said very softly. 'I want to never ever leave him. I want to be one of those things . . .'

'Things?'

'A monogamist.'

They married at the Register Office on the last day of August. Bambi wore a white miniskirt the size of a little apron and a hat of white ribbon with a white spotted veil. The office had made up a collection and bought them a sherry decanter and glasses. I could not imagine that Bambi would ever serve sherry from a decanter; but I donated my five pounds perfectly pleasantly. Philip had made his choice and I hoped, but I did not expect, that they would be happy. They honeymooned in Greece.

Bambi never came back to work, she was busy at their new home. She wanted to start a family at once. She was making curtains, painting walls. Philip came to the office with a streak of white gloss in his hair and laughed when someone commented on it. For a month he looked like a man half-drunk. He laughed easily, he walked faster, he left the office earlier every day as if he could not wait to go home. He was sentimental about court cases, especially those involving young women. He suggested that we pay all the clerks more. He irritated all of us unspeakably.

It didn't last. By autumn his tan and his look of incredulous joy had both faded. I wondered what it was like for him, to go home to Bambi when he was tired and irritable from a difficult day in court, wanting someone to talk it over with, and finding instead a pretty child in paint-stained leggings wanting him to go out and get fish and chips for supper.

He had agreed that they should have the baby she wanted. But she did not conceive easily. He never mentioned it but Bambi herself telephoned me once or twice and said that the nursery was painted, the ducks stencilled on the walls and the carpet laid down, but no baby was on the way.

Then, six months after the marriage, on a wintry grey February day she came into my office looking pale and drawn. A Bambi lost in the cold snow.

'Can you do me a divorce, Miss Cook?'

I have trained myself to look calm and impassive but I think my jaw must have dropped. 'Bambi?'

Her rosebud mouth drooped. 'Can you do me a divorce, please? I don't want to be married any more.'

I straightened my pens beside my blotter. 'Why d'you want a divorce, Bambi?'

She gave a little shrug. 'He doesn't love me any more,' she said simply. 'He's cross all the time. He just kind of stopped loving me. I don't know why. I'm just the same, I think, but he has changed. He doesn't want me any more.'

I compressed my lips on my irritation. 'This doesn't sound like a job for a lawyer,' I said as patiently as I could manage. 'You must talk this through with Philip. People often have difficulties in the first years of marriage. You have to get used to each other, you have to adapt. You have to give and take.'

All the old clichés flowed easily enough; but Bambi's fair head just dropped lower and lower. When I finally finished she looked up at me. 'It's not like that for us,' she said.

'Like what?'

'It's not working at it and give and take for us.'

I had forgotten how irritating she could be. I uncapped my fountain pen which in the old days, when she had been Bambi the new temp, had been a clear signal for her to leave.

'I don't understand you, Bambi. But I *do* know that you will have to talk this through with Philip. You must explain to him how you are feeling, and then he will tell you if he has any difficulties, and then you must work together and resolve them. Then, if you cannot reach an agreement, after you have *really* tried, you must find another firm to handle your affairs.'

❖

She was not listening to me. She shook her fair head with a strange childish stubbornness. 'We got married for love,' she said. 'Not many people do that, you know. They think they do, but most people get married because they know each other really well, or because they're used to each other, or because they're afraid they can't get anyone better. Or because they like doing things together. But we got married because we were madly in love. Madly.'

I waited. None of this made any sense at all.

'So when we stopped being in love,' she glanced at me, '*madly* in love . . . there was nothing else.'

'What d'you mean, nothing else?'

She gave that sad little shrug again. 'We aren't friends, we don't like the same things. We don't *do* the same things. We don't even like the same food . . .'

I thought of Bambi's cream cheese sandwich lunches and fish and chip suppers, and Philip's preference for the best restaurants and the most elaborate service.

'So now he's not in love any more there's nothing to hold us together,' she said. 'There's no . . . glue.'

'Glue?'

'People marry for love but they stay together because it works for them,' she said, a wise child. 'They own things together and they do things together. They have children together and they bring them up together. People who marry their friends have thousands of things to do together and to talk about. But for us, there's nothing. All there was ever was being in love. And now that's gone . . . there's no glue.'

'Perhaps you can make love come back?' I suggested, sounding, even to myself, like an advice columnist of the most romantic type.

Bambi shook her little head again. 'Not love like that,' she said. 'Not *mad* love. When that's gone, it's gone forever. That's why I want you to do me a divorce.'

I pulled my legal notepad towards me. When she had worked in the office we had called her Bambi the Bimbo behind her back, and once or twice it had slipped out and someone had called her Bambi the Bimbo to her face. She had not minded. She had smiled that appealing defiant little smile and tossed her blonde head. 'I might be thick; but I'm cute,' she had said last summer.

Only now when I agreed to represent her for her divorce did I realise that she was wiser than I. She was wiser than Philip. She knew when something had started and she knew when it was over.

'I'm still glad I did it,' she said. She had her tiny handkerchief out and she blew her nose in it. 'It's good to be in love *madly* – just once in your life. Even if it can never last. Isn't it, Miss Cook?'

But I didn't answer, because I didn't know.

The Playmate

◆

She leaned forward against the constraint of the seat belt. 'I can remember it from here,' she said. 'The trees make a tunnel, a tunnel of green. When I was a little girl we used to sing from here . . .' She sang 'Under the spreading chestnut tree . . .' and broke off with a self-conscious giggle.

'But surely your home was always London?'

Imogen shook her head. 'We *lived* there – but I called Sussex my home.'

'And did you come down every weekend?' He was curious about her childhood, with that fey talented mother and the dull stockbroker father. The house in the suburbs had been the father's house, furnished in his style; but the little cottage belonged to the mother. The father hated the little terraced farmworker's cottage set back from a mud lane in a row of red brick, sprawling with roses and hollyhocks. He stayed away while the mother, a difficult, attractive woman, had furnished it eccentrically in a ragbag mixture of colours and patterns. She brought her easel and her paints and her little girl almost every weekend in summer, and once or twice – rich rare events – in wintertime too.

'Once it even snowed,' she said. 'And we went tobogganing on the Downs. I had a tin tray.'

'Your mother tobogganed?' he asked incredulously. She was dead now, a thin beautiful woman always wearing velvet in rich deep colours. She was old by the time he had met her. He had gone to her elegant London flat to interview her and fallen at once under her spell. Greatly daring, he had asked her if she would come out for dinner. She had looked at him long and hard – that deep dark blue provocative look of hers. 'I don't dine with young men any more. You had much better take Imogen.'

He had taken the daughter to please her – and to secure himself another invitation. Then it was a pattern; he would have tea with the mother and talk about art and criticism and gossip, and then he would take her quiet daughter out for dinner. He could not have said what made the older woman so seductive. It was not her beauty – though much of it still endured in the flirtatious turn of her head and the deep secretive blue eyes. It was not her wit, though she had an acid tongue and a fund of stories which made him laugh and long to have been part of her circle when she was the darling of the cosmopolitan art world. It was more the sheer female power of her. There was something toe-curlingly seductive about her, there was something that made you want to both tenderly cradle and powerfully crush her.

Imogen had inherited none of her mother's appeal. 'Dear little Midge,' he thought tenderly. He liked to think of her as she had been all those years ago – a little girl unsubdued by her mother's beauty and talent, sledging on a tea tray on the gentle slopes of the South Downs.

'Did you play alone?'

Midge glowed. 'No. I had a friend in Sussex, a special friend, my very own friend.'

'Who was she?'

'Not she. A boy. He came to do the garden, John Daws.' She smiled. 'Mother called him Jack – jackdaw you see. He was supposed to dig the garden but he used to play all day with me. Mother said she was hiring a gardener, not a nursemaid, but we didn't care. He would take me down to the stream to fish, or we would go and see the sheep or the calves. He let me bring the cows in for milking and play in the dairy, he took me to the mill to see the corn grinding. He let me slide down the chute for the grain and caught me at the bottom!'

'Your mother let you play with a farm boy?' He had to readjust his view of her. He would have thought her too fiercely protective of her daughter to let the little girl out without supervision. He would have thought her too snobbish to welcome a friendship with a farm boy.

'She used to say to him, "Fly away, Jackdaw!" – but then she always let him stay for tea. He would sit on the chair nearest the door and watch Mother make my tea. He would jump up all the time to fetch things for her, lift things for her. Mother liked to do her own cooking in Sussex, it was like a playhouse for her.'

'He came every day?'

'Every single day. Some days we all went out together, we'd take a picnic and he would carry Mother's easel and her paints. We'd go to the stream and the two of us would play while Mother painted. When it was wet we laid out a city out of bricks and cards on the floor and Mother sketched us while we played.'

'How old was he?'

'He was halfway between us!' she exclaimed. 'He was ten years older than me, and ten years younger than mother. I thought that was very special. I was seven, he was seventeen and Mother was twenty-seven.'

'And how old was your father?'

She looked surprised. 'Oh, we never thought about Father. I don't know. He was older – perhaps forty. You know how it is when you're a child. Everyone is either your playmate or a grown-up.'

'And John Daws was your playmate?'

She was suddenly serious. 'He was my friend, the only friend I ever had.'

'Have you kept in touch?'

'No,' she said slowly. 'I never saw him after I started boarding school. I started at twelve, and then Mother's work got so popular that people kept inviting her for the summer: the Riviera, or grouse shooting in Scotland one year.' She gave an unconscious shiver. 'That was dreadful.

All loud men and tall women and dead birds! Acres of tiny feathered bodies at the end of every day. More than anyone could ever eat.'

'Did you never come down to Sussex again?'

'She kept promising me ... but then she was ill, and Father rented the cottage out to pay for the nurses.'

'So you never said goodbye to John Daws?'

'We were children,' she said firmly. 'We didn't need to say good-bye. At the end of each weekend he'd just say, "See you next week then", and I'd just say "Yes". He'd look at Mother and she would smile at him, then he'd tip his cap and go.' She was watching the way the light flickered through the tall beeches on to the road. 'This is the long hill,' she said. 'D'you know, I dream about it still.'

'You must have forgotten him when you went to school,' he suggested. 'You must have made *some* friends at school.'

Imogen shook her head. The sunlight flickering through the trees gilded her brown hair and then threw her into shadow. 'No,' she said. 'I didn't fit in. I wasn't like the other girls and I didn't know how to learn. They knew about boys and clothes and pop music and I only wanted to get back to Sussex and Jacky Daws.' She hesitated. 'I was lonely.'

'Didn't you boast about him? You could have called him your boyfriend.'

'I wasn't that stupid!' she exclaimed. 'They would never have understood. They would have turned it into something ugly. He was private. He was my childhood friend, my only friend. I've never told anyone but you. You are the first friend I had since I lost him. I've never been back until now.'

'I hope it isn't going to be a disappointment,' he cautioned. 'John Daws will be grown up, they may have put a housing estate on your little village green.'

She shook her head. 'It'll be the same,' she said. 'And Jackdaw will be there, just the same.'

He said nothing, watching the road as they breasted the hill and gathered speed down the other side. The road was lined now with thick clumps of coppiced chestnut bushes, as impenetrable as jungle. The trees were a bright rich green. He felt the townsman's unease at the lush fertility of the place.

'Shall you mind if he is married?' he asked. 'Will he mind that you are engaged to me?'

She was shocked. 'We were children! It wasn't like that! He was my Jacky Daws. He used to wait for us to come by the lane end and when the car came round the corner he would jump up on the big running boards and laugh. He was reckless and quick and curly-headed and he would jump up on the car and laugh when Mother screamed. She always screamed a little bit – as a game. Then when we came in the house we would find the fire laid and ready to light and the tea all ready and she would say, "Oh Jackdaw! you are my treasure, my treasure!"'

'And then?'

'Then we'd have tea and he would take me out. We'd

go and see the pheasant chicks which his father was rearing, or a bottle-fed lamb in his mother's kitchen. We went on a long expedition to a barn and saw a barn owl's nest one night, we didn't get back till after dark.'

'Wasn't your mother worried?'

She shook her head. 'Not when I was with Jackdaw. And then I would go up to bed and I would hear them talking softly, so as not to wake me. It was lovely falling asleep in the little boxroom with the window open, and the smell of the flowers blowing in, and their voices whispering quietly in the room below. Sometimes he would not leave until the stars were out and the moon was shining, and I would hear them murmuring together, like sleepy wood pigeons cooing.'

'You loved him,' he said flatly.

She paused for a moment. 'He was the only person to ever make me feel important. No-one else really saw me. It was always Mother. It was always Mother that everybody loved. But Jackdaw was my friend. Just mine.'

'Until me,' he prompted.

She nodded. 'Until you.'

He wondered why the landscape seemed familiar: the easy arable country of mid-Sussex, the hedges thick with flowers and rich with bird life, the fields green with a colourwash of yellow. He realised he knew it from the mother's paintings. He had seen these fields, these very fields, a dozen times under a dozen different skies, in different lights. She had a great gift of making the most prosaic scene into an enchanted world. The shadow of a cloud on growing corn, the speckle of scarlet from poppies on a verge, all combined to give the impression of strangeness and yet familiarity. She had been a powerful painter, a seductive painter. He wished he had known her when she was twenty-seven as the farm boy had known her. He felt that if he had known her then, he would never have recovered. As it was, knowing her when she was old and facing her death, she had woven a spell around him. She had enchanted him.

'Right here,' her daughter said.

He signalled and turned the wheel and they were at once engulfed in the deep sweet-smelling green of a beech wood. She wound down the window and air blew in colder and damp.

'The river is at the bottom of this hill,' she said. 'We used to fish.'

The lane was narrow, winding between broad-trunked trees, splashed and speckled with sunlight filtering through shifting leaves. He had a swift glimpse of the river, a clear sandy bed with sweet water dancing over yellow stones, and then they were driving up the other side of the hill.

'Right here,' she said. 'At the little signpost.'

He could hardly see it. It was a fingerpost grey with lichen, leaning drunkenly backwards. It said 'Woodman Row' in letters which were half-eroded by time and weather.

'That's us,' she said as if she were coming home. She

put a hand on his arm to tell him to slow down and he realised that she was half-expecting a curly-headed reckless youth to sprint from the trees and fling himself at the car.

'He's a grown man now,' he said gently. 'Pushing forty.'

'Yes,' she said. 'Silly of me. I keep forgetting. Everything else is the same, you see.'

He drove slowly down the little track and stopped at the first cottage. She opened the car door and stepped out. There were four cottages. The end two had been knocked into one, which was marred by the bulbous lump of a white aluminium and glass conservatory stuck on the side. He saw her wince and then look down the road to the last cottage.

'Why didn't she leave it to you?' he asked. All the rest of the wealthy estate, the London flat, the paintings, the car, the exotic and expensive jewellery, had been left to her daughter.

'She left it to Jacky Daws,' she said quietly. 'That's how I know he's still here. The lawyers gave him the deeds. I just assumed he'd be here, living here. That's why I thought everything would be the same.'

He slammed the driver's door, and locked it. 'I thought we were driving out into the country for a picnic. I thought we were just having a look at the outside of your old home. You never said anything about meeting him.'

For once, she was not listening to him. She had opened the sagging garden gate and was walking up the path to the cottage. The front door stood open with sprays of honeysuckle peering curiously inside.

❖

'Now just wait a minute . . .' he said.

She tapped on the open door and then stepped over the threshold into the cool dim interior.

The door opened directly into the kitchen. A man was seated at the kitchen table: a stocky small man, with iron-grey curly hair. He had a sheet of newspaper spread on the kitchen table and parts of some machine spread out in their own little pools of dark oil. He looked up as she came in and then slowly rose to his feet, wiping his hands on a piece of rag.

'Why, Imogen,' he said gently.

'Jackdaw.'

They stood in silence, scanning each other's face and then he smiled a broad easy smile and waved her into a chair. 'If I'd known you were coming I'd have had something ready,' he said. He moved to the sink and filled a kettle and switched it on.

'This is my fiancé, Philip,' she said.

He nodded with a smile. 'I can't shake hands. I'm dirty.'

'I knew you'd be here,' Midge said. In the dimness of the cottage her face was luminous. She was smiling, her eyes were bright. 'I knew you would be here.'

He nodded. 'I guessed you'd come sooner or later. But I'd have had tea ready if I'd known it was today.'

'You always had tea ready for Mother and me,' Midge said.

He nodded. 'She liked it so.'

Philip cleared his throat, interrupted the slow rhythm of

[184]

their speech. 'Why did she leave you the cottage? It's a very valuable asset, isn't it?'

The man shot a swift warning look at him. 'She had no use for it herself,' he said gently.

'She could have left it to Midge. Or given it to a charity.'

'She liked Jackdaw,' the girl interrupted. 'I expect she wanted him to have it.'

The man nodded. 'She was generous.'

'Very generous,' Philip said rudely. 'The place must be worth something like £80,000. Rather a big tip for a gardener, isn't it?'

The man flushed, his pride stung. 'I wasn't just the gardener,' he said. 'I kept everything nice for her, I kept things safe for her. It was always ready for her to come back. I waited for her.'

'You waited?' Imogen asked.

'She never said she was not coming.' They could hear the hurt of the seventeen-year-old youth in his low voice. 'Every spring it was ready for her, in case she came. Every spring it was ready for her to come home. The garden, the house, and me – waiting for her to come back.' He paused. 'She asked me to wait for her.'

The kettle boiled and the automatic switch clicked abruptly off.

'You loved her!' Philip accused. He could not tolerate the thought of their intimacy, of their cooing like wood pigeons at night, of her asking him to wait for her. She had never asked anything of Philip, except to take Imogen to dinner. By the time he had met her she had gone far beyond him, far beyond all possibility of desire. He knew she had never looked twice at him. He faced the man as if they were rivals, knowing, in his sudden enmity, that they had both loved her. He found himself shifting his feet, squaring up to the older man as if the woman they had both loved was still alive. As if she might ever have been won by either of them. John Daws looked quickly from Philip to Imogen as if he wanted to understand where this sudden rush of aggression had come from, then he looked away, his face guarded.

There was a long silence. Outside a jay scolded abruptly and then went quiet. John Daws said nothing. He turned back to Philip as if he understood, as if he recognised a mutual pain.

'She was a good employer,' he said.

Imogen rose slowly from her seat, her eyes fixed on John Daws. 'Did you love her?' she asked. 'Did you? Was it her, all the time?' She scanned his face as if she could see the bright seventeen-year-old who waited at the corner for the sound of his mistress's car, who waited, and waited, although she had forgotten him altogether. Imogen was staring as if she could see the only happy days of her childhood breaking and reshaping into a new pattern, a pattern of betrayal. Days in which she had not been the centre of love but had been a diversion, or even worse than that ... an alibi. An innocent chaperone whose presence made an adultery possible.

Imogen gave a quick painful gasp. 'Why,' she cried in the thin voice of a shocked child. 'Jacky Daws – you were not *my* friend, you were *never* my friend! You were her lover! You were her lover and never my friend at all.'

He said nothing. He bowed his head to her as if to confess to the betrayal. Then he raised his eyes and scanned her hurt face.

And both men waited with fear for her to look towards Philip when she finally understood.

Going Downriver

I started this diary with a view to publishing it alongside my thesis. I thought I would call it something like 'Living with the People – a year with the Nloko' and that there would be a picture of me on the front with Shasta and one on the back of me on my own outside the hut they gave me. My diary was, in those early days, rather self-conscious, perhaps a little self-satisfied – I'd accept that as a criticism.

I had in mind a woman reader: a rather bright anthropology student in her first year, say. I addressed her frankly – as an expert – and I charmed her. I showed her my commitment to understanding a native people, and the stripping away of my western values. I showed myself in bad lights too: the meal of the maggots eggs, and the time they took me swimming; but there is a sort of golden glow over it all. It reads, I suppose, as the account of an adventure by an adventurer who knows he will make it safely home. Behind it all was the awareness of my apartment in New York, and my hopes of publication, my ambitions in the university, and my certainty that among all those young women readers would be one – or indeed more than one – who would be so impressed by my diary (and the pictures on the back and the front) that I would be 'set up' when I got back to NY after my year in the back of beyond. This may sound crude; but in all fairness when a man has been away from home comforts for three hundred and three days he starts to be a little edgy and to long for a darkened bar, a Budweiser, and a woman with long legs sitting on a bar stool.

Not that I am celibate. Far (very far!) from it. I live in the best hut in the village, re-thatched especially for me, with Shasta: a stunning beautiful bare-breasted Nloko woman. Her nose is too flat for Caucasian taste and her hips are broad and plump, which the Nloko in their natural wisdom admire; and we do not. But she is a princess of this people, which makes her choice of me rather flattering.

We went through some kind of ceremony. Unfortunately I was not at all fluent in Nlokoese and much of it was beyond me. But I think we were, in their terms, married. How to explain to her when I have to leave is a problem that I shall worry about when I go. One of the charming aspects of the Nloko people is that they have no sense of distance or time. They have no words to describe time beyond weather descriptions such as sunrise, sunset, or, at the most distant future, the next rains. They cannot plan long-term. So to explain to Shasta that marrying me was a mistake because in a year I would leave her and never return was quite beyond *my* command of the language, and *her* concept of time.

To be honest, she was very pressing, and very seductive. What with the ceremonial drink, and Shasta perfumed, oiled and painted, I was pretty much of a goner. When I woke up and the ceremony was done I was in my hut, oiled, painted and perfumed myself, with the brown and beautiful Shasta spilled across my bed. It was too late to argue, and besides she awoke with a smile so gentle and trusting that I could not resist the temptation of holding her, and stroking her smooth brown legs and waist, and then I couldn't resist making love to her again.

To be fair to them, the whole ceremony – as well as everything else they do – is based on consent. No-one may coerce any other person. Every decision of the community has to have the willing and verbal consent of every individual. This sounds idyllic. Actually it's incredibly time-consuming and inefficient! It's only because they have such a small community – about fifty people in this village – and because they do things by tradition that things ever get agreed and performed.

At the 'wedding' the rule of consent applied. And they did ask me, very slowly and clearly, if I consented to being her husband. And I must say, in fairness to them, that before I passed out from the drink I said, 'Yeah. OK. Why not?'

I don't regret it. It could not have worked out better. Shasta's status as Princess has given me unique access to the Nloko people, who trust me and confide in me and actually come to me for advice. It has made the thesis as easy as writing this diary. I am investigating puberty and coming of age among the Nloko, and I have been besieged with their beliefs, taboos, and individual experiences. Nothing has been hidden from me. I know every secret. I could have wrapped up the thesis a couple of weeks ago. But the boat only comes upriver every four months, so I have to wait until my appointed departure time two months or so from now – fifty days to be precise, allowing ten days to travel downriver by canoe to meet the government launch.

I have not exploited Shasta, it's a relationship of feeling. I've never seen anyone light up in the way that Shasta does when I come near her. I've never had a woman wash me from head to toe for the sheer joy of touching every part of my body. I've never had a woman sit still, like a rock, for three hours just because I fell asleep one lazy afternoon with my head in her lap and she would never disturb my rest. It's heady stuff! I've even had thoughts of sending the manuscript home by the launch and staying here, and letting the career and the apartment (and even the willing female anthropology students) go hang. But to be honest I'm too ambitious, and too intelligent, to get stuck here.

It palls after a time. In the first few months I was awe-struck by their relationship with their world. They eat well and live well in this wonderfully constructed and organised village, without leaving a mark on the forest around them.

When you see them hunting they almost *become* trees and shrubs. When you see the children playing at the river edge they are as much a part of nature as the fish in the water and the parakeets shrieking in the trees overhead. Their whole world revolves around the hierarchy of the village in which women and the women's religion is totally dominant. This produces a wonderful serenity about the place. The women are the keepers of the wisdom and the health of the people. The men support them, respect them, obey them – and they have their own sub-culture of brotherhood and comradeship. I haven't cracked that, to be honest. But it doesn't bother me. At home I'm not really a guy's sort of guy. It's too competitive for me. I like the company of women, I like the admiration of women. The Nlokoese women treat me with a respect bordering on awe – I'm lapping it up!

I imagine I shall miss Shasta like hell. I don't think even the most liberated anthropology student will be as abandoned as Shasta is with me. She makes love as if it were some glorious ceremony which builds slowly and elegantly from one smooth sinuous movement to another. And then finally, when you can hardly bear the controlled beauty of it any more, she throws her dignity away and she is an animal, a beautiful animal, in her passion.

It doesn't take a PhD to know that this kind of experience is rare. I shall break my heart without her, I know it already. I expect when I take the launch downriver I shall feel like throwing myself overboard rather than leave her. And I'm concerned for her too. I have tried to discover what happens when a wife of the Nloko is left by her husband. Shasta's beauty, her passion, her wonderful grace in everything she does will not last for long. You only have to look at her mother, pot-bellied, round-faced with twinkling sarcastic eyes, to see where my lovely girl is headed. She should have married one of her own kind who would have stayed with her and grown fat and sarcastic with her. Instead she chose me, who has adored her, and been adored by her: a year of absolute passion, instead of a lifetime of conventional comfort. I know what I'd choose.

But I don't know what she would choose since she cannot imagine our parting. I told the whole tribe when I arrived that I would be leaving in a year – when the rains come again. And they all smiled and nodded reassuringly. '*Ralende,*' they said softly. Which means, as far as I can translate, 'of course', or 'naturally', or 'it has been ordained'. So she ought to know that I am going, even if she never mentions it and always behaves as if we will be together forever.

I am, of course, taking sensible precautions. I use contraceptives both to protect her against pregnancy and to protect us both from diseases to which we might not be naturally immune. I would ruin my academic reputation if I left behind any major damage to the Nloko tribe. A western disease, or a half-caste child would be professional death for me. Also, I think that Shasta could remarry if she has no child. Something one of the women said suggested that she had been married before. I asked the woman, one of Shasta's aunts, what she meant by the word I understood as 'the previous husband'. Shasta snapped at her, and the other women seemed appalled at some kind of lapse of taste. I said nothing more, but that night I asked Shasta if she had been married before. She laughed. 'Many, many times,' she said. And then she sat on my lap and kissed me. 'But you are the best of all.'

August 18

I was disturbed this morning to find that my chest of personal goods has been touched. More importantly, the supplies of contraceptives have been stolen. Theft is practically unknown among the Nloko so I am hoping that one of the children has taken them for playthings and that Shasta will get them back for me, despite her dislike of them. She complains that they are against nature – the nearest translation would be 'blasphemous'. I think she would like to conceive my child. But no, lovely seductive Shasta. No chance. Whatever your feelings we will use western contraception, and until I get the packet back I shall sleep cautiously beside my princess, refusing to touch her, even though she cried last night for a caress.

I have finished the final interviews for my thesis and much of it is already written. I experimented with a new introduction today, but I shall leave the conclusion until I get back to New York and feel settled enough to look back, to 'recollect in tranquillity'. They could not have helped me more. I think every day one of the boys or girls of my research sample – eleven- to fourteen-year-olds – has come to the hut door and squatted outside to be my companion for the day. Rarely has any anthropologist had the honour of being a prince among his research group! They call me Prince Rainbringer, and I am thinking of that as a title for the diary. I have no idea how much travelogue-type books can earn, but I am spending the imaginary royalty cheques in my head! I *must* have a big gas-guzzler car, and get a better apartment.

Indeed, as the time comes for me to leave, I am longing for my homecoming. I long for a properly cooked steak. My mouth just fills with water at the thought of donuts, coffee, chocolate, a Big Mac. I am going to pour junk food down my throat when I get home. All we have been eating here for the last few days is river fish and cassava bread, for breakfast, lunch and dinner, as preparation for the great feast to celebrate the coming of the rains.

I shall be sorry to miss it. It had taken place just before I arrived, and it will happen again just after I leave. It's obviously central to their religion, which is typical primitive Pantheism. They believe that all growing things have a spirit life, and that the seasons change as they wish. The big transition from the dry period to the rains has to be assisted with a ceremony and a major sacrifice. Shasta will be officiating. I asked her, rather frivolously, if they had a special rain dance, but she smiled and told me it was *'sere'*, which means a mystery. She is particularly attractive these days, withdrawn and thoughtful. It is costing me a good deal in self-control not to make love with her, especially as I am going away so soon. I want a farewell fling. Last night she begged me to kiss her, just to kiss her and nothing else. I really thought I had better not.

August 28

It has happened. I suppose it was inevitable really. Shasta is powerfully seductive and I am a young man with normal appetites. I had some hope of being able to withdraw in time but her arms were tight around my back and her legs wrapped around my hips. It makes no major difference to me. Nothing can delay my departure and if my good luck holds, any baby she conceived last night will miscarry, or die young. As with most primitive peoples the infant mortality here is fairly high. If it survives I hope it won't be too white. I don't want the child to be uncomfortable, of course; but more than anything else I don't want some callow young researcher with no idea what it is like to be out in the field for a whole year to come along and see a half-caste child and start the kind of gossip that would ruin my professional reputation.

I know that they have knowledge of plants that can cause abortions. I patted Shasta's flat belly and asked her to make sure there was no baby. She laughed delightedly and said, 'ralende', 'it is ordained', so I suppose that's that. It's her

◆

decision, so she will have to carry the can. There is certainly nothing *I* can do. The marriage and the child has been quite beyond my control and no-one could expect me to sacrifice my chance of success and wealth in New York for a voodoo marriage and a half-caste baby.

She has painted her belly with a spiral concentric pattern in a deep orange dye. She looks breathtaking. The ceremony of the rains is obviously one which absorbs her to the exclusion of everything else. She still sleeps in my bed and services my every need but she has an inner restraint which I sense. Can it be that although she refuses to understand the concept of the future she does in fact know that I am going away? Very soon actually. Only another month.

September 23

I have some plastic bags for my precious research papers and this diary and I have packed all but this book and pen carefully away. Shasta sealed them with sap from a tree rather like a rubber tree. She assures me it is waterproof. She is helping me prepare for my departure. She's in a cheerful optimistic mood. I was dreading this stage, thinking she would be clinging and demanding, so I suppose I should be pleased that she sets about finding my old rucksack and packing my few clothes and souvenirs with such contentment. Actually, I can't help feeling a bit peeved.

They have set up a large oblong table on a huge wooden trestle for the ceremony of the rains and draped it with flowers and leaves. Shasta, who is now painted from her dark upswinging eyebrows to the very soles of her feet, often walks around the table, humming softly to herself, for all the world like a suburban housewife checking the place mats. I ran up the little ramp to the high table and slapped her warm butt the other day and she led me away and said, *'Dourane'*, 'Not yet', very sweetly. Since then I have treated it as the holy of holies and stayed well away.

Shasta's serenity and quiet joy seems to be reflected in everyone else. Everywhere I go I am greeted with smiles and often little gifts of flowers or fruit. I don't doubt that I'm being wished bon voyage, and I have taken a thousand photographs of everyone before sealing up my camera and films in waterproof packaging for the long journey downriver. They have no objection to photographs now – though I had to insist when I first arrived. But everything seems to be permitted to me now. I caught myself caressing the smooth thighs of Tharin, Shasta's younger sister: a girl just deliciously at the brink of womanhood. She smiled and let me touch her and I had the sudden heady sense of being able to do anything in the world that I want here. I took her by the hand and led her down towards the river. If she had hesitated for a moment I swear I would have stopped, but she followed me smiling, trusting like the little girl she is; a little dappled doe in the flickering shadows. I am ashamed to say that I had her, and she was a virgin. I tried to make her promise to say nothing; but she was in pain and bleeding a little and she just waved me away. I only hope that there will not be two Caucasian-Nlokoese babies born to the tribe next year. I shan't go with her again. It's too risky.

My only major regret, as I pack, is not being able to record the ceremony of the rains. But to be honest, I can't bear to miss the launch. It would be another four months wasted for the benefit of recording a drunken all-week hen-party conducted in a language I can only just understand and for a religion which is incomprehensible to the western mind. I suppose if I were a better scientist I would make the sacrifice and stay. As it is, I cannot bring myself to delay. The bright lights are calling me! I could drink a lake of beer! And I really want a woman of my own colour. Shasta's love and her passion and tenderness have been a great gift. I won't forget them. I'll probably dedicate the book to her. But right now (and this is *not* for publication!) I want a long-legged girl to talk dirty!

September 26

Something very strange and disturbing has happened. I was working at my little table in the doorway of the hut when I dropped my pen top and bent down to pick it up. I then saw, at the foot of the king-pole of the hut, a piece of cloth poking out through the tamped-down earth. I took my penknife and scraped around it and it seemed to be some kind of plastic-wrapped package. I was angry for a moment thinking that it was one of mine which Shasta had stolen as a souvenir, but when I opened it I found it was not my writing, and it had obviously been buried for some time. The most amazing thing is that it is a chapter of anthropological research notes and a couple of grainy photographs of Shasta with a middle-aged, rather unattractive Caucasian male.

My first thought was for my own thesis. It would be hopelessly redundant if this bastard had been here first. I couldn't understand it. I'd done a total search of all publications and I couldn't imagine that someone had published work on the Nloko that I had missed. The tribe's entire attraction for me had been that no-one had lived with them before. I'd get them fresh.

He'd been working, predictably enough, on rites and ritual. There was a whole load of notes on primitive fertility rites – I've no time for that sort of thing. It seems to me to be hardly worth the paper it's written on. Who cares if they crush fruit to make the rains come, or kill fish, or cut the throats of monkeys? What difference does it make? My kind of research is immediately applicable to social science in the US. Puberty, how to manage it. What are adolescents like in a natural world? That kind of stuff. Solid research in its own right and very, very sellable.

I blundered out of the hut with the notes and snapshot in my hand and bumped into Shasta's aunt, who was shelling beans at the foot of the feast table. I waved the photo under her nose and asked her, 'Who is this man?'

I was surprised by her reaction. She jerked back at once

and I could see, under the painted spirals and the dark skin, that she had gone pale. She muttered something very softly and then she tried to take the photos and the papers away from me. I tugged back, and then finally I pushed her hard, so that she had to let go. She sat down with a bump and I asked her again, while I had the upper hand, 'Who is this man?'

She said that word again – previous husband. The word I had heard before. Previous husband. But she said nothing more. Neither my shouts nor, I'm ashamed to admit, a threatening fist, got another word out of her.

I stamped back to my hut to sit on the sleeping board and think. There *had* been another anthropologist here, and he had lived in this hut, my hut. And he had probably slept with Shasta. And then he had gone. But why hadn't he published? And why hadn't he taken his research notes? I knew that I would never be parted from *my* research notes. So maybe something had happened to him, in the forest or on the river. Maybe he had gone out one day, taking a break from work, and had an accident, and now he would never publish and never make money and never sit in an attractive office at a good college with a sexy secretary to make the coffee.

I shivered. I looked out of the open door of the hut to the dancing ground in the centre of the village and the ramp and the big trestle table covered with flowers and fruit. I suddenly wanted to be safely away, with my feet up on the rail of the launch and a can of cold beer in my hand and all the well-kept secrets of the Nloko tribe, worth a fortune to me, safely in a briefcase in my cabin.

September 29

They are giving me a tremendous sending-off party. I am officially recognised as the father of Shasta's child and a man of great potency and a prince in my own right. 'Prince Rainbringer'. All the women have made flower chains for my neck and I am required to strut around the village while they throw petals at me and sprinkle perfumed oil wherever I walk. I am consenting to do this to oblige Shasta. She has made it unusually clear that if I do *not* play my part then there will be no canoe to take me downriver. I feel manipulated and resentful towards her. But she is at the peak of her beauty and confidence and she does not seem to notice. If I were staying then we would have words and I would give her a timely introduction to patriarchy. But since I am going I might as well leave graciously. After all, I have not done at all badly out of this. I am taking away the work which is going to make my fortune, I have escaped infection and, although I have made her pregnant and possibly her little sister too, I seem to have got off scot-free without any payment or punishment.

They keep giving me the strong drink that I had at the wedding feast and it's going to my legs. I've had to sit down at my little table and I'm writing this while the women dance. Before my eyes they're just whirling colours.

It's a most wonderful sight: exotic, barbaric. If my things were not all safely packed I'd take another photo, except I don't think I can see straight. I have a vague idea of bringing a camera crew back here and making a documentary. I'd be good on television. I've got those sort of looks. That's probably a good career plan for me. A wider audience, and a bit of glamour to go with the academic work.

I'll have the lot. As soon as I can get out of here. I went to Shasta just now and asked her about the canoe and she gave me her sweetest smile and showed, by the wave of her hand, that when the sun starts going down I will set off. The boatmen prefer travelling at night, despite rapids and crocodiles and piranha fish and water snakes. Still, I'll have to trust them. Anyway, since the princess is all dressed up in her ceremonial gear, and I am pissed out of my brain, I can't argue.

It is growing velvety slowly dark. I have danced, I have drunk. I have been kissed by a thousand women. I had two, roughly, greedily, one after another in my hut where Shasta and I used to love like angels. Everything seems to be permitted to me. I slapped the second one around a bit and found that I *adored* seeing her flinch even while I was lying on her. So I guess that's something else new that I have learned during this trip – and also not for publication! My legs have totally gone now. They have laid me on the table and heaped me with flowers. Actually all my muscles have gone, except my hands. I've never been so drunk in my life. Shasta, as some funny joke, has laid my diary on my chest. I'm still scrawling while they dance around me but now my fingers are getting numb. She leans over me, she asks me if I wish to ride down the river in the canoe? Do I, Prince Rainbringer, consent to go to the water? I say, 'Do I hell? Yeah, yeah, yeah. Let's skip the ceremony and go.'

The women danced around the table until the huge mango moon came swiftly up over the dark canopy of the forest. The man was slipping from sleep into coma when they lifted the cover from the table. The trestle was a beautifully carved canoe. The princess helped them to lay him in the canoe and then took up her knife. She slit the spine of the diary and slashed the pages into ribbons of white which she sprinkled gently all around him. Then she leaned over him once more, and kissed his cold lips. Then she drew her knife slowly across his throat.

Singing quietly, the women lifted the canoe and slid it down the bank into the river. They waded out beside it, Shasta with them. Singing, with their beads chinking quietly, they thrust the canoe out into main channel of the river where it spun once, like a compass needle seeking direction, and then the water took it and it moved swiftly, smoothly down river.

Shasta waded back to the bank and raised her arms out wide to the river to thank it for the gift of the man and his seed, and for their chance to make another truly noble sacrifice for the rains. As she threw back her head and raised her voice there was a deep echoing thunder from the dark skies above her.

The rains began to fall.

The Other Woman

❖

I did not know that Andrew was having an affair until I found the note from her to him in his jacket pocket. And then I knew almost everything, all at once.

I knew that she worked in his law company, because she had written to him on the company memo pad. I knew that she was stylish, because she used a fountain pen and a special pale blue ink. I knew she was confident and well-educated, because her handwriting was bold and large, with a little dash over the i's rather than a dot. My own writing is small and spiky and shows that I am anxious about putting pen to paper. I don't always know what to say, I am afraid I will write incorrectly.

She wears a perfume I don't recognise. I put the note to my nose and had a little sniff. It smelled musky and expensive. I imagined that it came in a dark green box with a bottle of real glass, twisted like a barleystick. I even nibbled a corner of the paper as if I would learn something about the taste of her. Then I spat it out, feeling stupid.

I knew that she was fairly senior in the company – the

casual use of the memo pad and the fountain pen told me that. I guessed that she was single – the company isn't too keen on married women at senior levels. I thought that she would be beautiful. Andrew has never dated any girl who was not strikingly attractive; except me. I was only ever pretty, seven years younger than him, pale-skinned, blue-eyed, fair-haired. Our families are neighbours in Scotland. I was in love with him when I was five and he was an infinitely superior twelve. Everyone had always thought that we would marry. When he came home from London, qualified and with a good job, we did. I had just failed my A levels. It was what I had longed for all my life.

I imagined that this woman would never have married the first and only love of her life. I imagined that she would have gone to university, like Andrew, and trained, like Andrew, and now she would command a good salary and have freedom and independence. She could have anything she wanted.

Maybe she wanted my husband.

I reread the note. It said:

Darling,
  Bruised but happy.
  What about dinner at my place? 8pm tonight.
Just us.
  V

I listed in my head the number of things I knew from the note. She was confident enough to call him 'Darling' – unless of course she was one of those gushing women who call everybody darling. But I didn't think so, not if she were senior in Andrew's formal traditional law company.

She was 'bruised but happy' so their lovemaking must be rough and joyous. As I thought of this, I had to go to the toilet and throw up. Then I had a glass of water and went on thinking.

'Dinner at my place' indicated that she was single, or at any rate had a place of her own where she could entertain a lover. '8 pm tonight' confirmed her efficiency, and also showed her command of Andrew. He couldn't just drop in at her place after work. He had to go when he was bidden, at a proper time for dinner. This was not the note of a woman who was being used in a casual affair. It was the note of a woman who was secure.

'Just us' made me feel, if possible, worse than 'bruised but happy'. 'Just us' indicated that there could have been others. That V and Andrew were a recognised couple. That they entertained other people at her place. This was not a hurried hidden liaison. They were public. They were confident. They were 'us'.

And if Andrew is a half of 'us' . . .

What am I?

That question kept me thinking all the time from lunch, when I drank another glass of water, until it was time to collect George from school. I walked through the park to the school gates and waited outside in the sunshine with the other mums. A friend said I looked a bit peaky and I smiled and said I had been overdoing it in the garden: the weeds.

Then George came out and I could go. While he watched children's programmes, bouncing on the sofa in the sitting room, I spread the note out on the kitchen table and read it again.

I wondered what the V stood for. Verena? Victoria? Surely not Violet? I remembered that Andrew had a company phone directory by his desk in the workroom where I do my sewing and George has his Scalectrix laid out on the floor. I went into the room, stepping over the race track carefully, and looked through the directory. There were a lot of names, it took me half an hour to look all the way through. But I found her. Valentina D'Arby, corporate tax specialist.

Valentina.

I thought of what it must be like to have been christened Valentina. It's as if she started her life with a promise of glamour. My name is Heather. They could not have chosen a more ordinary name for me unless they had called me Grass.

D'Arby. I wondered if she really was D'Arby, or if she had the nerve to rewrite her name from Darby to D'A. I thought Valentina would have the wit and the guts to do that. And the D'A was very stylish.

Corporate tax specialist.

I closed the directory and went and made George's tea. I could not even speculate about what Valentina D'Arby did as her work. She was as far beyond reach of my imagination as if she had been head of MI5. I simply could not think what she would do in the office. I could imagine her clothes easily enough: dark business suit, cream shirt, maybe a brilliant flowered silk scarf thrown over one shoulder and pinned with a brooch. I could imagine her desk: dark wood, and two phones on it – I was sure she would have two phones. A plant in the window, perhaps an orchid which would never go brown at the leaves because someone had forgotten to water it. Cream carpet. Bendy-legged steel chairs. A book case with big corporate tax books in it.

George had Space Invaders on toast for tea and then we played Jumping Frogs, a new board game which he had for his birthday. I let him win. He had his bath and went to bed without protest. He's always tired on Thursdays after games.

And all the time I was heating up Space Invaders, and failing to see the dangerous move in Jumping Frogs, and wrapping my son in his bath towel and hugging him tight, I was thinking about Valentina D'Arby and what she would be doing at this time of day.

I knew I should feel angry. It's such a cliché – the note in the pocket; like lipstick on a collar, or a bill for flowers. But I didn't feel angry. I didn't even feel surprised. It was worse than that. I had somehow been expecting it ever since we had married. Someone said on our wedding day: 'He's a real high-flyer, Andrew.' I had thought then: I am not a high-flyer. I am not even a low-flyer. I am a kind of pony and cart person. I'm not a big achiever. I don't even want to be. The evening I had just spent: caring for George, cooking him Space Invaders, playing a silly game with him, and getting him into bed at the right time without a conflict, truly seemed to me the best way to live. Or at any rate, it's the only way I know.

◆

I wondered what Valentina D'Arby would have made of it.

Andrew did not come home that night. He was not due home for three days, he was in Brussels on business. He rang me every morning at nine o'clock our time. It's eight o'clock on the continent then. Or maybe it's ten. He asked after George and he asked me if I was well. I did not say anything about the memo from Valentina D'Arby. I didn't even ask if she were in Brussels with him. I didn't want to hear him lie. I didn't want to hear the truth.

Instead I rang his office. I felt strange and shaky dialling the familiar number but asking to speak to Miss D'Arby. The switchboard girls know me but I put a tea towel over the phone like they do on the television when they want to disguise their voices. I could hear the telephone ringing in her office. I imagined her reaching for it. Today in my imagination she was wearing a brown suit with a coffee-coloured shirt. Her long dark hair was swept back into what they call a chignon. I don't know exactly what that is, but I know Valentina D'Arby would know. And she could make her hair do it, too.

The phone rings.

She reaches out for it. She picks it up. Her nails are *very* well manicured and shiny with pale polish. She says ''Allo, Valentina D'Arby.'

She is foreign!

I am so surprised that I forget to put the telephone down. And so I hear her say it again.

''Allo, Valentina D'Arby.'

[212]

She has a low steady voice, she sounds exotic. She might be French or she might be some nationality whose accent I don't know – Polish or Armenian, anything. I put the telephone down and I find I am blushing furiously with an inexplicable rush of warmth to my face. I never thought of her being foreign but it fits exactly with the smart Italian suits and her dark hair.

I stop myself abruptly and turn to the sink to wash up George's breakfast cereal bowl. Of course, I don't really know that she wears tailored suits. I don't know that she has thick long dark hair. But I am unaccountably excited about how much I *do* know. I know her name. I know her extension number. I know she is foreign. I know she is my husband's lover.

Half the morning, while I am making the beds and Hoovering the carpet, I wonder where she learned to speak English, and where she trained in corporate tax. I feel almost certain that she must have gone to an English university, whatever her nationality. Andrew's firm is very traditional. I can only imagine them employing a foreign woman if she was trained in England. I feel absurdly light-headed and excited while I pull the cylinder Hoover behind me through all the upstairs rooms. I lug it downstairs and stow it in the cupboard under the stairs. I cannot resist going to the kitchen telephone again.

I dial the number, I wrap the tea towel around the mouthpiece. I ask for Miss D'Arby, and then I hear once again her quiet, assured voice: ''Allo, Valentina D'Arby.'

When I say nothing she says: "'Allo? Who is this?'

And for one insane moment I want to say: 'It's me, Heather!'

But I say nothing. I put the phone down slowly, with immense regret.

It rings almost at once and I snatch it up, certain that Valentina D'Arby is phoning me. But of course it is not her. It is a mother from school. She wants to know if I have remembered that George is to go to tea with her son today. She will collect them from school. I will fetch George from her house at eight. She says, 'What will you do with a free afternoon?'

And I say, slowly, 'I think I shall go to London.'

I have done something I think enormously clever. I saw it done once on television. I have sent Valentina D'Arby a bouquet of flowers to her office. Now I am watching the front door of the office, a large plate-glass building with a revolving door and a windy open pavement between the door and the car park. She will come out of the door carrying my flowers and I will see the flowers and know her. I will know the woman who is having an affair with my husband.

I chose the flowers with care. Silly really, for they are nothing more than a device to trap her. But when I was in the shop it seemed to matter. I did not want to give her roses or carnations, they are too obvious for her, brash flowers. I chose only yellow and white freesia, and a few miniature white iris with tiny yellow tongues. An exquisite bouquet, I know she will like it. She is bound to take it home, especially on a Friday evening. She would not leave it in the office over the weekend.

I wait in my car, scanning the front door of the building until six, I am starting to get anxious. Perhaps she will work late, or perhaps she has left early to see someone. Then I see the glint of reflections as the plate-glass revolving door turns and a woman comes out carrying my flowers.

She is smaller than I imagined, less striking. She is wearing the sort of suit I had thought, only it is navy blue. She has navy shoes too, with low heels. She doesn't carry a handbag at all, she has a black leather briefcase instead. I think that is *intensely* smart. Her hair is brown and glossy as I imagined but cut in a neat bob, curling under at her shoulders. She is walking straight towards me.

I am frozen behind the wheel of my car. She is walking directly towards me and I am sure that she can see me, and see through me. She knows it was me on the phone, wanting to hear her voice. She knows it was me who sent her flowers to trap her. My fingers grip on the wheel and my mouth drops open. I look, I am sure, like some pale girlish fish, gulping against the glass wall of a tank.

She walks straight past my car. She comes so close that the tail of her jacket brushes my wing mirror. Her car is parked two rows behind mine, facing in. I watch her in my mirror. She has the keys in her hand. Her car unlocks when she presses a button. It is a sleek two-seater, navy like her suit and shoes.

Suddenly I want to speak to her. I am sure that I won't
be able to follow her when she is driving in the city that she
knows, in rush-hour traffic. If I am to attract her attention it
has to be now, here.

I get out of my car and I run through the rows of parked
cars towards her. She is about to reverse her car out of the
parking slot and does not see me. I call her name but she
does not hear me. Like a fool I run straight towards her
car, I step out from the other parked cars, and the back of
her car knocks me from waist to knee, knocks me and
throws me down on my back with a horrid clunk and the
exhaust gases burn my face with their stink, and I scream.

I am in her office. It is as I imagined, only the carpet is
grey, not cream. She pours me a brandy, from a decanter
in the cabinet. She has a first-aid box open on her desk and
she has patted my grazes with antiseptic cream. She has
touched me with extreme gentleness, lifting my cotton
summer dress and dabbing very softly each little graze with
a ball of soft cotton wool. I feel as if I have been kissed all
over by her delicate little touches.

'Do you want to call the police?' she asks. Her English
is perfect with just a slight intonation. 'I was quite in the
wrong. I simply did not see you.'

'No.'

She hesitates. 'Or a lawyer?' she asks. 'I accept, as I say,
full liability.'

I shake my head.

'I am sorry,' she says. 'Perhaps you are in shock. Should I take you to a hospital? Or call a doctor?'

I shake my head.

She finishes her gentle tending of me and she pulls down my skirt.

'Then may I call your husband?' she asks. 'You should not drive yourself, I think.'

'No,' I say. 'My husband is Andrew Wade.'

There is a moment of total silence. She looks at me as if she would read my face. I suddenly realise that although her eyes seem to be dark brown there is a rim of gold around each black pupil.

'Then I have hurt you twice,' she says slowly. 'And there is no apology I can make.'

We stare at each other as if we would learn every detail of the other's face.

'You are not how I thought,' she says.

'How?'

'I imagined someone smaller, more ordinary.'

I gesture awkwardly to my rather washed-out summer print dress and handbag swollen with oddments. 'I'm very ordinary,' I say.

She shakes her head. 'You are physically brave,' she said. 'And impulsive, and imaginative, and . . . beautiful.'

I say nothing, trying to absorb this information. 'I used to be pretty,' I say hesitantly.

She shakes her head. 'You have the looks of an English rose. A pale beauty.'

'You are just as I imagined,' I say. I feel shy, like a younger girl at school talking to a prefect. 'I imagined your clothes. I even imagined your office. It's just as I thought.'

Her face lights up as she laughs. 'Corporate power-dressing,' she says dismissively.

We are both silent for a moment.

'What did you come here for?'

I can feel myself colouring, the warmth of my blush spreads up from my collar bones to flood my face with heat. 'I came to see you.'

She sits in the chair opposite me, she crosses her long legs. She takes a cigarette from her briefcase and lights it with a table lighter. I watch her, quite fascinated. Andrew hates smoking, he hates women who smoke.

'Obviously. But why? To ask me to stop seeing him?'

I shake my head.

'No,' she says. 'You look too complicated for such a simple gesture.'

'I just wanted to see you,' I said simply. 'I found a note from you, I was imagining too much. I was making pictures of you and him in my mind. I couldn't bear not knowing.'

She nods, flicks the ash off her cigarette. 'I too,' she says slowly. 'I have imagined him with you, and your son. At weekends, when I am alone, and when you go on your holidays, I imagine you then. I tried to see you as fat and dull, a drag on him.'

I blink at this cruel caricature. 'I knew you would be beautiful, I knew you would be as you are.'

She nods. 'So he has two women who know their place,' she concludes. 'Night and day. Home and away. Wife and mistress.'

'I wasn't surprised,' I volunteer. 'I wasn't surprised when I found the note.'

She blows a smoke ring, I have never seen anyone do that except on the television. We both watch it. It has the fascination of George's bubbles that he sometimes blows in rippling streams from a bubble tub in the garden.

She nods. 'I was not surprised when he told me he would never leave you. He has chosen the right women, it seems.'

'I have to go home,' I say. 'I have to collect George . . .'

'Can you be late?' she asks. 'Could you come out for a meal?'

'He can stay overnight with his friend,' I say. 'But I never thought . . .'

'Phone them,' she says. She moves to the desk and picks up one of the telephones. 'Let us see where this chance meeting takes us. Phone and make the arrangements, and we'll go out to dinner.'

I move as if I am dreaming. I call and say that I will be late and can they keep George? Susan is happy for him to stay, and she teases me about my assignation in London. I say: 'No, no, an old school friend.' And I think: what am I concealing?

We drive in her car to a restaurant. The waiters know her and greet her by name. The food is quite wonderful. I eat with George so often that most of my meals are child's food: baked beans, fish fingers, sausages. With Valentina I eat asparagus and then cold smoked salmon, and zabaglione for pudding. She orders a very cold bottle of wine, dry and strong. I don't drink usually, but I love the taste of this.

I feel rich. When they bring us coffee and a glass of aromatic dessert wine I feel full and wealthy. There is a mirror behind Valentina's dark head and I can see my reflection. I am rosy with warmth. I am smiling.

We have talked all through the meal. She explained about her work and I told her about George and his first days at school. How empty the house seems without him. She told me about her girlhood in Padua – I will look it up in George's atlas when I get home. I told her about the hills behind Perth and the cold red-bricked house where I lived all my life before Andrew came to take me south to London.

It is getting late, I should go. I have to drive home.

She calls for the bill and won't let me share the cost of the meal. She shrugs. 'Company expenses.' She puts down a gold card.

She drives me back to my car, standing alone in the car park.

At the moment of leaving I am suddenly awkward. I do not know quite how to say goodbye.

'I doubt that we will meet again,' she says carefully.

I shake my head.

'I hope George goes on liking school,' she says. 'He sounds such a lovely boy.'

'I hope that Gleeson and Sons do their tax your way,' I say politely.

She laughs. 'I will end it with Andrew as soon as he comes back from Brussels,' she says easily. 'Please don't worry about it. I give you my word.'

'I hope it doesn't hurt you,' I say. It is ridiculous, I know, that I should fear for her loss when it is my husband who is her lover. But I am thinking of the demanding office routine and an empty flat at the end of her day. Her beautiful clothes in the silent bedroom, the immaculate cold kitchen. The empty tasteful sitting room. 'I didn't come to make you end it,' I remind her. 'I just wanted to know . . .' I tail off. I am not sure what I wanted to know about her. Everything, I suppose. I had a great appetite to know all about her. And now I know, I am not satisfied. I feel, for some reason, sorrowful.

'I have wanted to see you too,' she says quietly. 'I am glad that you came, and we spent this time together. You have showed me what I am not.'

'What d'you mean?'

She shrugs. 'Women make choices that men never face. You will never have a career, you will never be a senior executive. I will never bath my son and put him to bed. I am glad to have seen you. It makes me value what I have set aside.'

'But you could have a child.'

She smiles. 'And *you* could be a corporate tax specialist,' she says. 'But we both made other choices. Perhaps we made our choices too young. But now we have to live with them.'

She leans forward and she kisses me on one cheek and then on the other. As her dark smooth hair brushes against me I can smell her faint warm perfume.

'Goodbye,' she says.

Andrew called into the London office before coming home and she must have told him then that the affair was over. He was tired and quiet at tea, though he played football with George for half an hour before bedtime. He came up behind me and put his arms around me while I was washing up and laid his head against my back. 'It's good to be home,' he said. 'I have missed you.' He had bought me some lace in Brussels and as he unpacked his suitcase he tossed a bottle of perfume on the bed. 'I picked that up for a colleague's wife, but it was the wrong sort,' he says carelessly. 'You might like it, darling.'

I looked at the dark green box and at the glass bottle twisted like a barleystick inside. And then I knew the last unknown thing about Valentina. The name of her perfume and how the bottle looks on her dressing table.

I slept that night wearing her perfume, in my husband's arms. But I woke in the darkness of the night and I saw her face and her hair as dark as the shadows. And I felt something I never felt before.

A sort of longing.

The Visitor

Eleanor opened the door to what appeared to be a forest –
a huge swaying fir tree pressed towards her, its topmost
fronds thrusting towards the ceiling, its broad skirts forcing
her backwards into the narrow hall where its branches
pushed against the pale walls.

'Not here! You've made a mistake!'

Still the tree came on, until it was fully inside the apartment. At once the place was filled with a rich disturbing
perfume of pine: a dark wintry smell, a smell of promise,
of excitement, as heady as new-made wine, the irresistible
secret life of evergreen plants in mid-winter.

'I've not ordered this,' Eleanor said. 'You've got the
wrong address.'

The tree stump thumped down on to the expensive vinyl
flooring. There was a brief shower of pine needles which
fell with a pattering sound like rain.

'Now look!' Eleanor exclaimed.

The tree leaned sideways and an old man looked around
it, through the thick branches, at Eleanor's angry face. He

was a short plump man, dressed in jacket and trousers of an indeterminate rusty colour. He had thick walking boots and a shapeless baggy hat.

'Eleanor Lease?' he asked.

'Yes?'

'I *am* glad!' He beamed at her, offering his hand. Reluctantly Eleanor shook it.

'I brought you this. Something made me think you might not have a tree yet.'

'We never have a tree,' she said.

His face fell like a disappointed child. 'You don't?' he asked. 'Why ever not?'

Eleanor made a gesture that took in the flat, its pale washed walls, the smooth neutral floors, the expensive ceiling-to-floor curtains which framed the iron-grey view of the river. 'It wouldn't go,' she said lamely. 'And I don't want the work, dropping needles and having to water it . . .'

'I'll water it,' he said firmly. 'And a bit of mess doesn't do any harm. I'll sweep up.'

Eleanor had a strong sense that she had lost control of the conversation, and Eleanor never lost control. 'I don't think you quite understand,' she said, her voice very cold. 'My husband and I have not ordered a tree, and we don't want a tree. We never have a tree or any Christmas decorations. We're not Christians, we think that Christmas has become absurdly over-commercialised. We never even have a turkey . . .'

'No turkey?'

She shook her head.

'No mince pies? No Christmas pudding? No stockings, no presents? No decorations? No carols? No candles in the windows? You poor child!' he exclaimed. 'Why on earth should you deny yourself these things?'

Eleanor glanced around the flat, as if its pale stylish décor would answer him. 'I think we're rather too sophisticated for that sort of charade.'

'Sophisticated?' He said it as if it were the name of a rare and perhaps fatal disease.

'Yes.'

He shook his head. 'My poor girl, my poor girl.'

Eleanor opened the door a little wider. 'I'm very sorry but we don't want your tree. And now, I'm very busy, so perhaps you would go . . .'

'But I'm here to stay!' he announced as if it were delightful news. 'I've come for Christmas! I'm Robin's Uncle Nicholas, from the old country.'

'What?'

'That's why I brought the tree,' he said. Gently he leaned it against the wall and wiped his hands on his disreputable reddish jacket. The tree filled the little hall with its powerful green presence. 'It's my little gift. To my hostess.'

'Rob didn't say,' Eleanor protested faintly.

He chuckled. 'Because he didn't know!' he exclaimed. 'A surprise, you see! I just had a sense – you know how it is – that it was time the two of you had a visitor, and had an old-fashioned Christmas.'

Eleanor briefly closed her eyes. 'Would you like a cup of tea? And I'll telephone Rob. He's at the gallery right now. But I know he'll want to come straight over.'

She showed the unwanted guest into the living room and seated him on the white leather sofa before the broad panoramic view of the river. A light sleet was blowing against the picture windows and the overhanging sky was grey. The steely colours of the view matched the white and off-white of the living room. This room had once been featured in a house design magazine as the most coolly elegant in London; and Eleanor and Rob had never changed it since that day except to get everything dry-cleaned, almost continually.

Eleanor telephoned from the bedroom, so the old man could not hear her. 'Rob? You'll have to come here. There's a man who says he's your Uncle Nicholas, and he thinks he's staying with us for Christmas.'

There was a brief astounded silence.

'My who?'

'Your Uncle Nicholas.'

'What? My mother's cousin? We used to see him all the time when we were kids.'

'Well he's here now.' Eleanor kept her voice low. 'And he's brought the most appalling vulgar tree with him.'

'A tree?'

'An enormous Christmas tree. He clearly thinks he's doing us a favour. It's huge and bushy, and it . . .' Eleanor broke off. She could not put into words how disturbing the tree was, how its passionate green life seemed to challenge and contradict the little apartment where everything was made from plastic, or vinyl, or steel. It was as if the old forests which had grown here long before bricks and concrete and cement had suddenly broken through and were alive and powerful in the very heart of the city.

'I'll come straight away.'

'Good,' Eleanor said shakily, and went back into the living room. The old man was standing opposite the window and tapping the wall with strong firm taps. When Eleanor came in he turned and beamed at her. 'You've got a fireplace here!' he said. 'I'm sure of it! Listen!'

He tapped along the wall and the dead sound of thick plaster suddenly echoed.

'We boarded it over! We have underfloor heating. We don't need a fire!'

'You need something alive in the room,' he said. 'A little movement, a little colour. Something to come home to – a place for the cat to sit.'

'We don't have a cat,' Eleanor said.

'No,' he agreed. 'Such a pity. But a fire is a companion in a way.'

'I don't need a companion,' Eleanor said. Even to herself her voice sounded thin and lonely. 'I have my work, and we go out most nights.'

'To see friends?'

'Business dinners, and private views, that sort of thing.'

'Well you're young,' he said as if to comfort both of

them. 'And soon there will be babies coming along . . .'

'We don't plan on children,' Eleanor said abruptly. 'We don't like them.'

He looked shocked. 'You don't like children?'

'Oh, I don't *dislike* them,' she said hastily. 'But we don't want any. We don't feel the need! There's my career: I'm a freelance corporate designer, and Rob has the art gallery. We're too busy for children, and . . .' She looked around the white sitting room with the grey curtains '. . . we don't have a lifestyle that children could fit into.'

'No,' he agreed. 'They tend to make you fit in with them.'

There was the sound of the key in the lock. 'Oh Rob!' Eleanor said in relief as he came into the room.

They had parted on a quarrel in the morning, and usually they would not be speaking. But this was an emergency.

'Hello,' Rob said. He crossed the room to Eleanor, so they faced the stranger together.

'I doubt that you remember me,' the old man said. 'It sounds as if you've forgotten everything you ever learned.'

'Are you my Uncle Nicholas?'

The man grinned. 'Little Robin!' he said. 'And I was afraid that the two of you were a lost cause!'

'Now, I understand from Eleanor that you have nowhere to stay,' Rob started.

'Oh I have, I shall stay here.'

Rob laughed his professional laugh. 'I wish you could. But unfortunately we don't have a spare room.'

'There's the study,' he suggested.

Rob shot a swift look at Eleanor which accused her of showing the awkward old man around the flat. She shook her head. 'I need the study for my work,' she said.

'No you don't,' the old man said acutely. 'You've got no work at all over the Christmas holidays – nothing till February, actually.'

Rob looked at Eleanor again.

'That's true,' she admitted reluctantly. 'But something could come up at any moment.'

The old man shook his head. 'It won't,' he said decisively. 'Companies are trying to save money, they won't bring in freelance designers like they used to. Times are changing.'

This was so close to what Eleanor had been thinking recently that she gasped.

'So I'll sleep on the sofa in the study,' the old man said.

'I don't really think . . .' Rob started.

'Till when?' Eleanor demanded.

The old man smiled at her as if it were all agreeably decided. 'Twelfth night, of course,' he said.

Dinner was surprisingly pleasant. Eleanor and Rob usually fetched a take-away, or microwaved a ready-cooked meal from the delicatessen on the rare nights when they were both home. But while they were hidden in the bedroom, having an anxious whispered discussion about their unwelcome guest, he started cooking in the little white and steel galley kitchen. Saucepans which had been chosen only for their shiny high-tech looks, were taken down from their carefully designed places on the wall, onions were frying, steaks were sizzling. By the time that Rob and Eleanor had emerged from their room, the kitchen was glowing with candlelight and redolent with the smell of steak, onions and new-made bread.

'I thought I'd cook you a good dinner,' he said. 'To say thank you.'

Eleanor wanted to say something cold and cutting about the mess in the kitchen, but there was hardly any mess. She wanted to complain about the apartment smelling of cooking, but the scent of the lightly fried onions and steak was too good. He waved her to a place and she sat down, Rob opened a bottle of good red wine, the old man placed a plate of steak and sweet onions before her with a green salad on one side and warm new-baked bread rolls on the other. '*Bon appétit!*' he said.

He was a good companion. Rob and Eleanor usually sat in silence or read magazines or newspapers at the dinner table, but this evening they enjoyed talking and listening. Uncle Nicholas had been all around the world; he had a fund of anecdotes from every country. And he drew them out to talk. Under his gentle prompting Eleanor found that she was talking about her childhood, about her powerful rebellion against her family that had driven her from Bolton to a London university, and from there into design work, when she had met Rob. Uncle Nicholas nodded, as if her exile from her childhood home and family explained much. 'But what has happened to you, Robin?' he asked. 'When you were a little boy you loved colour and shape. I always thought you would be an artist, perhaps a sculptor?'

Rob grimaced and Eleanor suddenly saw that he was no longer a young man. For a moment he looked as grey as the kitchen walls. 'I didn't dare,' he said. 'The gallery seemed a safer bet, and now I make thousands of pounds on every piece I sell. Other people's sculptures. Other people take the risk and have the joy of making the things. I only sell them.'

Eleanor heard him with a chill sense of the passing of time and promise. She had always thought that the gallery was a way for Rob to fill in time, while he prepared for some beautiful work of his own. But he had not carved a thing in ten years. Somehow he had passed from being a young man who might do anything, into a man who ran a gallery, and would never do anything more. And she? She had slipped from being a young woman full of ambition and commitment into a woman who would design whatever a company ordered. She was a woman who could lay grey on white on off-white and think that it was an agreeable environment. She had forgotten the deep rich colours of passion and certainty: of birth and death.

'Pudding,' Uncle Nicholas said cheerfully. 'That's what we need now.'

From the oven that had previously only ever been used for reheating meals from the restaurant delivery service, he drew a dish topped with golden sizzling sugary crumbs. 'Plum crumble,' he said.

The smell wafted across the kitchen like a serpent of temptation. Eleanor smelled the sweet delicious perfume of stewed dark fruit and the crunchy hot topping. 'I really can't,' she said reluctantly. 'I have to watch my weight.'

He put the dish on the table and poured golden yellow custard from the saucepan into a jug. 'We need to build you up,' he said firmly. 'There's nothing more important than that now.'

Eleanor had thought that the first dinner must have been a lucky fluke. The old man, as a new arrival, had been on his best behaviour, soon they would be irritated by his presence and overcrowded in the small flat. But as the days wound down towards the Christmas holidays it was not like that. He continued to be opinionated, wrong-thinking, old-fashioned, eccentric; but she found him companionable during the day. He insisted that he cook a meal every night, and that she come with him to shop for food. He led her down alleyways to fruit and vegetable markets that she had not even known existed, just around the corner from the flat. He took her to little shops where people greeted him by name and stocked the fresh produce that he liked. He took her to stalls where geese hung swinging from their necks, where tangerines – brilliant orange against the foil of their wrappings – were like jewels encased in silver. He bought holly in great rich bunches of green, sharp with yellow thorns, starred with berries of red. He bought cascades of waxy white mistletoe berries and showed her the thin pale leaves as tough as angelica. He insisted that they buy pounds of cranberries, a fat wax-paper-wrapped bowl of a Christmas pudding, bright vulgar wrapping paper, make-your-own cracker kits, indoor fireworks, candles, and chestnuts for roasting.

There she stopped.

'How on earth are we going to roast them?'

'Now don't get upset,' he implored. They rounded the corner and she saw the builder's van parked outside their apartment block. 'I took the liberty,' he said gently. 'That room does cry out for a fireplace. Think of it as my Christmas present to you.'

In panic, she raced up the stairs and threw open the door, but she was too late; where the smooth white plastered wall had been, was a wide generous opening rimmed with brass. They had a fireplace.

Eleanor moaned in horror.

Tactfully he ushered the builders out of the flat and produced a wood basket filled with logs and pinecones. 'You mustn't expect too much at first,' he warned. 'But I happen to be a bit of an expert in chimneys and this is a good one. As soon as it warms up it will draw wonderfully.'

Eleanor retreated to the sofa and drew her feet up under her. She pretended to look away from him, at the view of the river; but the room was reflected in the iron grey glass and she could see him, rubbing his hands at the chaos he was causing, laying a fire, setting a match to it, and then sitting back on his heels.

'*Do* look,' he invited.

The room was transformed. Instead of the grey and white the leaping firelight laid a patina of gold and bronze on everything. Eleanor caught a glimpse of herself in the grey-tinted mirror and saw that she was glowing, as if sun-kissed: glowing and rosy and warm in the firelight.

'Say you like it!' he insisted.

She wanted to tell him that the new hearth would have to be filled in again. That they could not be bothered with the work of a real fire, that they were people whose apartment had always been a fashion statement – and that the fashion was for minimalism, coolness, greyness, neutral tones. It could not possibly ever be gold and bronze and flickering light.

But she found she was smiling, flowering under the warmth, like a golden crocus that comes out of the darkest coldest earth on the most unlikely of wintry days. 'I like it,' she said helplessly.

Rob when he came home saw the firelight first, the flickering live warmth of it, on the cold vinyl floor of the hall. The whole apartment which had been a palace of ice was now glowing with a radiant warmth and scented with live pine. Then he saw the reflection of the firelight in Eleanor's face which was warm and smiling. She looked as she had not looked for months, and Rob forgot the prestige of their off-white apartment, and forgot the critical appraising gaze of his colleagues, forgot too that what they had wanted was an austere look: a home in the colours of snow.

'Gosh, you look cosy,' he said, and flung himself down on the floor beside Eleanor and drew her to him, and smelled the perfume of her warm skin, the hint of smoke in her hair, and the delicious smell of roasting chestnuts,

'The builders found this,' Uncle Nicholas said, observing their sudden warmth with each other. 'In the chimney breast, boarded up and hidden.'

He produced a small worm-eaten piece of wood, bleached like driftwood, but stained in small wavery grooves with blue.

Rob received it into his hands. 'It looks like a figurehead,' he said hesitantly. 'How odd.'

Eleanor turned in the circle of his arm and stroked the rounded head of the wood. 'The bit that comes out of the prow?'

'Yes. But look, it is a woman and she is holding something.'

'Is that her gown?' Uncle Nicholas asked. 'That blue?'

Rob ran his finger down the groove of her gown. It still held a trace of a bright beautiful blue. 'It is,' he said wonderingly. 'D'you know, I think it is a Madonna. And she is holding a child.'

Uncle Nicholas said nothing, he just watched the couple on the other side of the fire, and when Eleanor put out her hand he sighed very gently, as if something very important had been accomplished. Eleanor stretched out to touch, not the smooth time-worn face of the Madonna, not the line of blue of her gown, but the tiny shaped form of her wooden baby at her breast. Eleanor's hand cupped the baby's head, as if she longed to feel a pulse in the little skull, and warmth beneath her palm.

'I shall restore this,' Rob said gently. 'I can take some time off, I shall get some teak oil and some wood, and I shall restore this. And when I have made her as good as I can, I shall get some wood for myself and I shall carve. I should like to carve a Madonna and child, like this.'

Uncle Nicholas waited, but still Eleanor said nothing. For a moment he thought he had yet more to do, but still she touched the child and her face was suddenly open to hope.

It was the morning of January 6th and Uncle Nicholas, Robin, and Eleanor were having breakfast in the cramped little galley kitchen of the apartment. Eleanor was not eating, she was drinking tea. She said she felt queasy and odd.

'It's too cramped here,' Robin said with sudden impatience. 'I need a workroom, and a woodstore. I can't carve on the sitting-room floor, I need a workspace.'

'A studio,' Uncle Nicholas suggested.

Robin checked at the thought. 'We could never afford one in London ... but perhaps in the country?' he said. He glanced at Eleanor, she was sipping her tea with quiet concentration. 'Are you all right?' he asked tenderly.

'I just feel a bit funny.'

Uncle Nicholas rose to his feet. 'I think my job here is done,' he said comfortably. 'I'll wish you a happy creative new year.'

'You're not going?' Eleanor demanded. She had a sudden pang of impending loss. 'You're surely not leaving?'

He nodded. 'It's twelfth night and I am finished here,' he said. 'Maybe another year.'

He walked out into the little hall and grasped the tree like a dancer, around its supple waist. A shower of needles pattered down, but neither Eleanor nor Robin minded.

'We've got so accustomed to you being here . . .' Robin began.

'You know how to cook now,' Uncle Nicholas observed.

'Oh yes.'

'And you have a proper fire . . .'

'Yes, but . . .'

'And you are starting to sculpt again, and you . . .' Uncle Nicholas turned with a sweet smile to Eleanor. 'You're going to find you have plenty to do.'

'You needn't go,' Eleanor said. 'Robin's mother comes back to England this week, why not stay with us till then?'

The tree swayed as he lifted it from the pot. Robin held the door. 'Happy New Year!' the voice came from the centre of the tree. 'A Happy New Year to all of you, dear children.'

The tree brushed through the doorway, and they watched him carry it down the stairs, shedding a scented trail of green. Then the door below banged, and he was gone.

The telephone in the flat was ringing. It was Robin's mother, she had come home early.

'Oh, you've just missed him!' Eleanor exclaimed in disappointment. 'And we have had such a strange time. Robin is sculpting again, and we think we may have to move house to find a studio for him, perhaps in the country . . . we have an open fire, and it has been so lovely! Robin has learned to cook, we had turkey this Christmas! Think of that! And I . . . I . . .' She broke off, she could not think of words to describe the odd sensations she was feeling: a queasiness like travel sickness, a tenderness at her breasts, a tendency to weep, a soaring inexplicable joy . . .

'Missed who?' Robin's mother demanded.

'Uncle Nicholas!' Eleanor said. 'Your cousin. He was here for Christmas.'

'I don't have a cousin Nicholas,' Robin's mother said.

Catching the Bus

❖

Jim was going to go to the Grammar. My mum had set her heart on it even though Dad warned her that Jim wasn't all that bright. She started saving for the uniform when he was nine, she said he'd need books and a satchel and a table and chair in his room to do his homework, and Stuart would have to go out and play while the homework was being done, and changes would have to be made. And my dad said: 'Don't set your heart on it, Maggs.' And my dad was right.

Jim failed his eleven plus, but all he wanted to do anyway was to go as an apprentice at Filton and build aeroplanes, and they would take him with a good report from the Secondary Modern; so he was happy. But then Mum kept the Uniform Savings Fund going because she had hopes that Stuart might suddenly change and not be football-mad and darts-mad any more, but be the one to put on the dark grey trousers and dark green blazer and go the other way to school – across the park and down the hill and all the way down to the Colston Road to catch the bus up to the

❖

Grammar instead of the Secondary Modern where everyone else went.

Stu didn't change and Dad said: 'That little nest egg of yours could put a new roof on the kitchen, Maggs. Shame to let it sit there.'

We had a kitchen which was just a little room out the back. It leaned against the house almost like a shed, and you went down a step to it and then from the kitchen into the back yard. It had a corrugated iron roof and when it rained it sounded like a marching band drumming. It leaked. That was why Dad wanted the Uniform Savings Fund for a new roof. When the rain came from the east it blew in, and set a little trickle of rusty red water running down the kitchen wall.

But Mum said: 'There's still our Lizzie.' And Dad said: 'What does a girl want to go to the Grammar for?' and Stu and Jim snorted with laughter and Mum said nothing.

But she didn't use the Uniform Fund for a new roof.

I was ten then; and I was bright. 'There's no point sending a girl to the Grammar,' Dad said to Mum very reasonably as he bolted the front door and she started slowly climbing the stairs to bed. I was in my room, torch quickly switched off, book hidden, pretending to be asleep. I was reading *Great Expectations*, which is about someone called Pip who is actually a boy, though I thought it was a girl's name.

'She'll get married and then it's all wasted,' Dad said as they went past my door. 'It's not as if she's going to do anything with it.'

Their bedroom door closed and I heard him moving around: the groan of the wooden wardrobe door opening and the jangle of the coathangers. Mum didn't reply. I heard the bed creak as they got in, and then the click of their light going off, plunging the house into comfortable dark. Then I switched on my torch again and turned the page.

Dad worked as a mechanic in a small garage on the main road. Mum did ironing. She said she'd never take in washing, she'd be ashamed to take in washing; but she could do ironing with her head held high. She said she liked it; but I saw her face when a washbasket piled high with shirts was waiting and she would bang the ironing board down on its legs and then heave it up to make it click into place at the right height. She had an electric iron with a green light in the black Bakelite handle which glowed as the iron warmed up, like an evil eye, keeping her on her feet when she was tired, making her bend over the board until late at night. The Bakelite was shiny and glossy on the back, black like the main road when it is wet. But around the green eye it was cracked and pale.

She had a special jug that I had made her in Art, and she filled it with cold water and dipped her fingertips in it and flicked them out over the white linens and creased cottons, and when the iron went over a fat resilient drop it hissed like a snake. The house was always filled with the warm scent of hot clean cloth, and one or other of Mum's hands was always stained with a little stripe of red where she had brushed against the iron and burned herself.

When I was tall enough to reach the board at its lowest setting I was allowed to do the handkerchiefs. First you went round the edges, the iron nosing its way round like a blunt-nosed explorer. Then you did the broad sweep of the middle, that was the best bit. Then you folded it in half and pressed the crease in the middle, then in a quarter and pressed down the quarter line. Big men's handkerchiefs went into three folds before they were halved.

'I love ironing,' I said to my mum.

'You wouldn't say that if it was all you could do,' she said.

I passed my eleven plus. 'I don't see that it makes any difference,' my dad said. 'What's she going to do with GCEs when she's married and with a baby on the way?'

'We'd have sent the boys,' Mum said.

'Boys need exams,' my dad replied inarguably. 'What does she want French for?'

My mum put down her iron, sitting it on its back on the board. The little green eye winked on as she looked across the room at my dad, eating his tea at the table. 'I've set my heart on it, Arthur,' she said. 'I've set my heart on it.'

Nobody asked me. They told me at school that I was a lucky lucky girl. But I didn't feel very lucky at home. When we had Sunday's roast beef in mince on Monday and then in sandwiches on Tuesday and then the bone boiled up for soup on Wednesday it was my fault, because I was going to the Grammar and shoes had to be paid for. The Uniform Savings Fund bought the blazer and the tie from the school's own second-hand stall, but there was still the PE kit and a special shoe bag to buy, and I needed a satchel and a felt hat with an elastic strap, and a hat badge in dark green enamel with the school crest on it.

Dad started to come home early on Friday nights and didn't have his pint any more. And then one day a big canvas holdall appeared in the hall, filled with a stranger's dirty laundry, and I knew my mum was taking in washing.

She bought a twin tub on the Never Never and it lived in the middle of the kitchen with one hose pipe attached to the tap pouring cold water in, and the waste pipe looped out over the sink pouring dirty water out. If you opened the lid when the washing was doing you could see the whole drum turning and shaking like some wild grey stew. There was a wringer fixed on the top and I turned the handle while Mum fed the clothes through the rollers before dropping them into the spin dryer. When the spinner was on, the whole thing juddered across the uneven kitchen floor as if it would run out into the back yard taking the damned washing with it. Then, when it had spun so long that the house had been half shaken to pieces, she opened the lid, heaved out the long ropes of laundry, and hung them out to dry on the rows and rows of new lines which my dad had put up in the back yard. Then she had to iron it, as well as the usual load.

The family chipped in. One of my aunts found a school satchel from somewhere, gave it a polish and presented it to me in August with a half a crown in the inside pocket. My Uncle Peter made me a wooden pencil case with my name in pokerwork on the inside. I was really pleased with that. My mum's uncle in Canada sent a postal order and that paid for the special games shorts and the daps. One by one the things were bought and put into the bottom drawer of the chest of drawers in my bedroom.

But there was always something more. I had to have special name tags. It wasn't enough to write your name inside things. They were specially embroidered name tags and they were three and six for a hundred.

'Three and six?' my dad said.

Mum nodded grimly, and bashed the iron down on somebody's collar.

It was my job to sew the name tags into my new clothes. It was my job to fold them and lay them carefully in the precious bottom drawer. It was my job, all through that summer, to tick off one item after another from the list the school had sent us, until it was the end of August, nearly the start of the new term, and the drawer was full.

'I only hope she's worth it,' my nan said to my dad. 'Seeing what it costs.'

My dad scowled. He never agreed out loud with my nan when she said something against my mum. But he had a special scowl and she knew what it meant.

'Throwing good money away on educating a girl,' my

nan said. 'What's she going to do with O levels? That's what I'd like to know.'

My mum suddenly appeared in the kitchen doorway. It was Sunday afternoon when my nan always came over for tea, and the ironing board was away for once and the twin tub pushed out into the yard. My mum was slicing bread and she had the bread knife in her hand as if she was Macbeth.

'She's going to have a chance,' she said. 'She's going to have *her* chance. She's as good as any boy, and she's got more in her head than Jim or Stu. They'd have had their chance if they'd passed the eleven plus, so she gets hers. And I don't know what she'll do with it, not French, or Maths, or Biology, or any of the things she's going to learn. I don't know what she'll do with O levels. But it's a step for her. It's the bus out of here for her. It's her chance.'

There was a dreadful long silence. Mum had never said a word to Nan in twenty years of nagging. She'd never said anything even to suggest that she thought there was anything more than ironing, and the row after row of houses all the same, and Sunday tea with Nan every Sunday, and a week at Minehead in the summer. She never said why she wanted one of us to go to the Grammar, and why she wanted it so much. She wasn't a woman who talked a lot. She wasn't a woman who burst out into explanations. She wasn't like someone in a book who is always explaining things, and feeling things, and saying some more. She just stood there with the bread knife in her hand, looking at Dad and Nan who looked back at her, and then she said: 'Tea in five minutes, lay the table, Lizzie.'

And I laid the table for tea while Stu and Jim and Nan and Dad sat in silence, maybe thinking about Mum holding the bread knife and suddenly saying that her daughter had to have a chance.

On Monday September 4th my shirt was clean and stiff at the neck. My tie was silky under my fingers. My blazer with the badge I had sewed on the pocket and my name tag I had sewed on the collar felt cool when I put my arms in the sleeves; that was the silky lining. My hat felt loose on my head, and the elastic strap was tight at my throat. My shoes shone like horse chestnuts, my satchel swung from my shoulder, empty of everything but my new pencil case and a purse, a special purse, even the purse had to be special: it was the school purse with a little zip and a strap you wore over one shoulder, with my bus fare inside. Because I wasn't going to the Secondary Modern within walking distance, on the other side of the park. I was going down to the Colston Road to catch the bus to the Grammar on the other side of the town.

My mum walked with me to the bus stop. She said she had run out of blue bag and she might as well get it now as later, and then she said she might as well wait with me for the bus to come. So she was there when I stood in the queue and waited for the green double decker bus to come round the corner, leaning as if it might fall over. And we didn't say anything, either of us, because there was nothing to say, now that I was there at last, at the bus stop, waiting for my bus.

My mum held her arms across herself, as if she were hugging herself in. Her hands were red from washing now, the fingernails and the cuticles white and soft from the hot water. She didn't reach out and tweak at my new blazer, or straighten my hat. She stood back a little, as if she just wanted to watch me go.

The bus came round the corner and the queue shuffled as it drew up. The conductor was standing at the foot of the stairs, his ticket machine resting on his stomach, his finger ready to press the bell. I glanced back at my mum and she was beaming at me, her face filled with delight as if it were the start of the summer holiday or Christmas morning. But her arms were held tight across her, as if she were hugging a baby which wasn't there.

I turned to the bus and I grabbed the pole and I jumped on to the step and I went inside and I found a seat on the scratchy seats with the zig-zag patterns and I waved at her through the dusty window.

And then I set off to get my chance.

Printed by RR Donnelley at Glasgow, UK